T0113398

KILLING COUSINS

A NEW YORK MYSTERY

ALEX MINTER

POCKET BOOKS

New York London Toronto Sydney Singapore

POCKET BOOKS, a division of Simon & Schuster, Inc.
1230 Avenue of the Americas, New York, NY 10020

Produced by 17th Street Productions,
an Alloy company
151 West 26th Street
New York, NY 10001

ISBN 978-0-7434-6332-4

First Pocket Books trade paperback printing September 2003

10 9 8 7 6 5 4 3 2 1

KILLING COUSINS

KILLING COUSINS

1 "Good evening, ladies," the doorman said. His voice had a boom to it, low and confident. He smiled and swept the two sisters from Texas, C. J. Wallingford and Maude Stowe, in through the revolving door of the Sutherland Hotel on Madison Avenue. It was a warm Wednesday evening at the end of September, just before midnight. The Upper East Side was as relaxed and cool as a healthy baby asleep in an antique crib.

"We've just been to see *Scarlet A,*" the women said, nearly in unison, to the deskman once they were inside. He was a tall man who wore a double-breasted blazer closed tight over his belly.

"Oh yes," he said, in a voice nearly as loud as the doorman's.

"It was terrific fun," C. J. sang out, with all the volume of someone who'd lost most of her hearing and didn't much care. "So much *edge.*"

"I hope the rest of your stay is as good," the deskman said.

The lobby wasn't large, and revelry could be heard through the vestibule that led to the Lido Bar, which had recently been adopted as the meeting place of a much younger set. A few of these smooth types had made their way into the reception area, where they lounged in groups of four and five on the sky blue velvet chairs that were arranged far from the windows looking out on the street. The ceiling here was dazzlingly white and low, creating odd echoes, so guests often said, "What's that?" when they weren't the ones being addressed at all.

"Carpet needs something," C. J. said as she and Maude moved across the lobby toward the left elevator bank, which was tucked behind a massive flower arrangement that leaned too heavily on petunias and freesia.

"Carpet needs a new carpet," Maude said.

"Didn't catch that," C. J. said. She was the heavier of the two. Maude wore a silver fox coat and C. J. had on a wide-lapel trench designed especially for her. Neither woman had brought her best jewelry to New York, though both wore their engagement rings, which were outrageous. They kicked at the carpet with the toes of their shoes and clicked their tongues when the worn fabric frayed underneath their weight, like the soft edges of their own memories.

A thin man in an inky blue suit and dark blue shirt watched their progress. He stood a few steps away from the elevators. He examined a poster of Sean Lennon, who was scheduled to play in a few nights at the Lido Bar. A smallish earpiece was attached to a cord that ran down into his jacket. He watched the ladies and nodded slightly, tucking his hands deep in his pants pockets.

C. J. and Maude passed over the disappointing carpet and arrived at the elevators. The thin man pressed the button, and the three of them waited together. Two elevator doors opened at the same time. The three of them got into one.

"What floor?" the man asked. He'd blocked their view of the buttons with his body.

"Eleven," Maude said. "Thanks."

The man pressed eleven and then penthouse. They stepped back. The elevator rose.

"What's that?" C. J. asked.

Maude looked at her and frowned.

"I didn't say anything."

The thin man looked at the instrument panel to the right of the elevator's doors.

"Sounded like 'Make it snappy,'" C. J. said. She frowned, rolled her tongue around in her mouth to catch at a bit of meat left over from the dinner they'd enjoyed at Swifty's.

Her perfume, handmade for her in San Francisco, filled the elevator with the smell of jasmine.

"No," the man said. "It was 'Make it sloppy.'"

He pointed at the plastic nodule that protruded from his ear.

"Oh, you've got something that speaks to you," C. J. said. She nodded to herself, as if this sort of thing would be more common in New York. "I've got a hearing aid, but it doesn't work worth a damn."

"In fact," the man said, "what you overheard were my instructions."

The elevator stopped at the second floor. The doors opened and closed.

"I don't understand," Maude said. She shrank back so that her shoulders rubbed the mahogany wall of the elevator.

"Make it sloppy. The first time I hit this place, I'm supposed to make it sloppy. These are my instructions." He smiled then, a leering smile that showed dark vertical lines around his mouth. Without turning around, he pressed the stop switch on the elevator and slipped a stiletto out of the breast pocket of his jacket.

"What?" Maude asked.

The man blotted out the security camera with a tiny can of white spray paint and then leaped up and smashed out several of the small lights in the elevator's ceiling. On his way down, he knocked the two women's heads together.

Because C. J. began to scream, the man attacked her before Maude. He slashed both women's throats and then grabbed C. J.'s trench coat, which he used to protect himself from the gushing blood. Now all was quiet.

The women's bodies sank to the floor. The walls of the elevator were splashed with crimson. The man flipped open the instrument board and forced the elevator to go to three, the laundry floor. He opened the door a few inches and slipped away. Inside the elevator, the blood rose. It pooled and ran out through the open door and into the elevator shaft with a degree of regularity, like a thin stream of water from a tap that has been carelessly left on.

It was calm in the lobby. The doorman came in and stood with Alexei, the deskman. They listened to the European dance music coming from the Lido Bar.

"I wonder how long those old Texas sisters have been coming here," Maurice, the doorman, said.

"Well, I'd say since I can remember," Alexei said.

"And you've been here . . . ?"

"Eleven years," Alexei said.

"Longer than that by a long way," Maurice said. "Because they were coming before I got here, and I've been here for twenty-three."

"And you've held the door for seven presidents, two kings, a princess, and a pope," Alexei said. A pimple had appeared on his neck, and he probed it with his finger.

They leaned on either side of the massive counter and were quiet for a few minutes. Neither man much liked the other, but over the years of nights they'd learned to ignore their feelings in favor of something like camaraderie. They breathed at about the same pace. Through the glass that separated them from the Lido, they watched the drunken young people snap at each other and laugh.

"Glad you shooed those kids back into the bar," Alexei said.

"They'll wander back in when it gets later and they get drunker."

"Something wrong with elevator six," Alexei said as he examined the electric board in front of him. "Looks like the power shut down or some such."

"Have Curly check it," Maurice said. "I'd rather stay right here with you."

"Ha," Alexei said. And then he phoned down to Curly in the basement. After the call the front lobby remained quiet, save for the occasional beep from the monitoring systems. Then Curly called back. And then all of the phones began ringing at once.

2 Felix Novak sat with Lanie Salisbury at the opening of a restaurant that had been something else only seven months earlier, when Felix had first arrived in town from Oregon. He hadn't liked the place it'd been, and now that it was something else, called Industrial Figment, he didn't like it much, either. He sat at one end of a banquette with some reporters and a tall woman he'd met several times before whose name was either Jane or Axe, maybe Jax.

Lanie had gotten Felix a black suede suit because of a story she'd done for *Manhattan File,* and now Felix drew the jacket tight around himself. He had no idea what Jax was saying. He put a foot up on the chair across from him and sipped his Maker's Mark, making sure not to spill any on himself.

It was then that Lanie got up and kissed a reporter from a rival paper. The reporter bear-hugged her and swung her around like a helicopter propeller, and club patrons ducked and yelled. The stranger let her go; she grabbed him by the ears and kissed his forehead. Felix took out a toothpick and brought it to his mouth, snapped it, and dropped it on the table next to his whiskey. Not much had been going on lately and he'd been thinking about leaving town. He wasn't happy with Lanie. He felt like she needed too much stimulation from sources that weren't him.

Lanie came back to the table and sighed, then sat down a foot from Felix.

"You want to break up?" Felix asked.

"No, I think we should stick around for a while," Lanie said. She was going through her purse. She pulled out some cash, a bunch of pens, her PDA phone, a couple of blueberry-and-granola bars. Felix watched her. Whatever she was looking for, she wasn't finding it.

"That's not what I said," Felix said.

"What wasn't? I'll meet you somewhere else if you're antsy. Not that I enjoy allowing myself to be beholden to your moods."

Felix nodded. He picked up his cowboy hat from the seat next to him and settled it on his head.

Lanie kept looking over at the doors. When they opened, she made a note of who had arrived on a Post-it pad. She breathed through her mouth and sipped a martini in a short glass. Her phone rang. Felix watched. At one time Felix had found all this terrifically exciting and attractive. More recently he'd been thinking a lot about repairing the fences on his mom's farm, back in Portland. Surely Joey, the hired guy, wasn't taking proper care. The only fences in New York City were made of iron. There was no real work for him to do here.

And he hadn't quite fit into city life, either. He didn't live anywhere, really. When he didn't stay with Lanie, he slept in his father's office on the waiting room couch. He kept his other suit and some shirts there in a closet. He wanted to be able to hop in his Roadrunner at any time and drive back across the country. Though he hadn't actually come close to doing that.

"You're not even on the party beat anymore. You're a big-time city hall reporter—what's the point of this free-lance page-eight bullshit?" Felix asked. "Isn't it beneath you to report for the *Sun?*"

Lanie glanced at him.

"I like to work; you know that," she said. "Talk to Janice or one of the other girls if you can't be nice to me."

"The model? I hung out with her last week at the opening for Bathhouse. She doesn't talk," Felix said.

"Sure, she does. She's getting a doctorate in comp lit at NYU. You don't listen is the problem," Lanie snapped.

Felix stood up slowly.

"Where are you going?" Lanie asked.

"Out of here," Felix said.

"Call me later, then," Lanie said. "I should be home before dawn. Hi, Billy!"

Felix walked to the front of the club. He smiled at the woman who was only called Janice. She smiled back. Comp lit, my ass, he thought.

Felix felt the doors close behind him. He turned right and headed west, toward nothing in particular. He loved this part, the walking around the city alone part. But he didn't smile. It'd been almost six months since Lem Dawes had been sent to Rikers for killing his little sister, Penelope. And Lem still didn't have a final court date. Since then Felix had done a few jobs with his father, Franklin Novak. They'd worked on corporate stuff, protecting disgraced CEOs who needed no protection, talking big to guys who would've been afraid if they'd only talked small. He spent the rest of the time watching and learning from Franklin's other two employees, Chris Gennardi and Philip Moyo, as they traced computer trails. Nothing big. He was ready for something new. And he was pissed at Lanie. She was never up for staying in, hanging out just with him. They'd never be able to fix fences together. Build a fire, cook up some rice and beans in a pot, and go to sleep next to the embers, wrapped in wool blankets. She'd go with him for a day, maybe. Then she'd be scrambling to get to her phone.

There was a good breeze going and it was warm out. Lanie said the gossip part of her job would cool down in October, that the city'd get duller then. Felix couldn't quite see her logic. And he didn't believe her, anyway. She'd warned him that he had to change his lousy attitude, and she wasn't the only one. He knew he had to get nicer; he just had no idea how to go about it. And it wasn't like his father could give him any tips.

He walked down to the West Side Highway and found his Roadrunner where he'd left it parked near some idle dump trucks. He got in and knew he'd sleep there, as he had on the first night he'd arrived in the city. He tipped his hat over his eyes and stretched out, tried to ignore the trucks rushing up the West Side. He wondered where Soraya was, but he didn't call her.

Franklin Novak lay in his bed with his girlfriend, Jenny Hurly. She chewed at the nail on her left pinky and stared at the ceiling. Franklin watched her jaw work. He enjoyed the way her messy raven hair looked, strewn against his white pillows. They'd only recently graduated to nights at his apartment, eschewing, finally, the regular room they'd used at the Gershwin Hotel.

"I could make eggs," she said.

She pushed the covers off her and he watched her breasts heave. He knew that she was like him, that neither had any idea what would come next or how serious they really were with each other. Would dinner with his son, Felix, be next? The idea seemed bizarre, though Jenny was a good eight years older than his son. There was that at least, thank God.

"If you want. But I'm not so hungry," Franklin said. He turned and kissed her on the cheek, pulled her close. It was past two in the morning and they both needed to be up early.

"Ever think about buying a plant?" she asked.

"It'd die. I don't even keep milk in the fridge," Franklin said. She smiled then and reached out and rubbed his bald head. Her lips were full and soft.

"Let me get you a plant—a ficus is always nice or a Christmas cactus. And sometime soon I'll make chicken potpie. Tomorrow night, if you're still free."

He kissed her. You're a lucky man, Franklin thought. And then he thought, Now keep saying it till you believe it.

The phone rang and he stood up to get it. Jenny grabbed the remote and flipped on the TV. Franklin moved quickly into the living room. He thought it might be his ex-wife, Ellie. She was back in Oregon now. After the last visit, when they'd properly said their good-byes to each other and their newly lost daughter, Penelope, Ellie had more or less threatened to come back at any time. Franklin had never quite managed to tell her that he was with someone else now and was happy. Probably because he wasn't sure if that was true. She had a habit of calling late at night, once she'd started in on the white wine.

He let the phone ring once more and caller ID told him it was Gennardi. Franklin picked up the handset.

"We have clients," Gennardi said. "It's a rush case."

"How'd they get to us?"

"They got your name from your old buddies down at Wackenhut. They want to see you in the morning, 10 A.M."

"Background?"

"Tonight about midnight, a double homicide in the Sutherland. Pair of sisters, rich. Their husbands are who you're going to see. They want you alone. It's all set."

"Great. I'll see you when I'm finished with them."

Franklin stared out at the slice of East River he could see from the living room window. He lived in a one-bedroom apartment in a twenty-year-old building on East Eighty-fourth

Street and First Avenue that was about as distinctive as a retirement home in West Palm Beach or an office block in Kraków. He liked it that way. He moved every two years and had almost no possessions save a bed, night table, lamp, couch, coffee table, chair, and some framed drawings that Felix and Penelope had made when they were little, before Ellie had left him and taken the kids out to Oregon. Before Penelope had been murdered in a hotel room. Before he'd taken Felix under his wing.

He found a bottle of Budweiser in the fridge and popped it open, took it back to the bedroom. The lights were out in there; the TV was off. The only sound was the buzz of late night helicopters coming in from the airports and honks from the tugboats down on the river. Then there was the rustle of Jenny under the sheets, curled in a ball, turned away from him. He stood at the end of the bed, sipped the beer, tugged at the hard round surface of his gut.

"I can't have dinner with you tomorrow night," Franklin said.

"Things were looking too good for us for a few minutes there," Jenny said, and her voice was muffled by the pillow.

He got into bed behind her, tried to spoon up to her, but her back was cold.

"Your ex isn't back in town, is she?"

"No. I've got a case."

"You better not pull the same shit you did last time."

"What's that?"

"Where you acted all hard and forgot that you love me."

"Which last time are we talking about? When my daughter was killed?" Franklin asked. He put the bottle on the night table and lay flat, looking up at the ceiling.

"I'm sorry," Jenny said.

Franklin didn't speak. He figured that he'd leave off calling Felix till the morning. Felix would call Soraya. She'd signed on for all the big cases. That was how they'd left it. Gennardi would already have been in touch with Philip Moyo, and they'd have started setting up from their end. Franklin knew he wouldn't sleep. He wasn't going to bother to try.

"Two old ladies were killed," Franklin said. "They were sisters."

"That's absolutely horrible," Jenny said. She shivered and turned over, toward him.

"Yes," Franklin said. "Murder usually is."

Soraya Navarro made her way through the ground floor of Eden-Roc. The place was packed with dancers and drinkers and she was psyched to be among them after a day of plodding through a paper on the writer Ama Ata Aidoo seen through the historical perspective of Simone de Beauvoir.

She waved at a new bartender who barely acknowledged her. Terrence Cheng still owned this place and Soraya's boyfriend, Gus Moravia, still worked for him, but things had cooled since Felix's sister, Penelope, had died. Drugs were no longer dealt at Eden-Roc. And no matter what she did, Felix, her oldest friend in the world, was still at odds with her boyfriend, Gus, because of his connection to what had happened to Penelope.

The club was still packed—but the people weren't from the city anymore. The hottest kids, the Japanese teenagers and the prep school kids, the secondary famous and the models and the makeup company heirs, and whichever rapper was just about to get their deal with Bad Boy entertainment, they were all elsewhere. Hotel bars were the thing now, but not Terrence Cheng's hotel bars. Those were flatlining as hard as Eden-Roc. Soraya didn't care—she only wanted to see Gus, have a quick drink, and get to bed.

She went down the stairs to the private lounge and found Gus hanging out near the deejay booth, sipping on a tequila with lime juice. He'd been drinking harder lately, but she hadn't said anything, not yet.

Gus kissed her once, then pulled away. He smelled of smoke, but that was probably just the club. The collar of his black suit seemed slightly off, wrinkled somehow, and he looked a little sweaty.

"What's going on?" Soraya asked. "Ricky at the front door just suggested I pay the cover. I told him I never paid a cover in my life and he said I should start thinking about it. You and him get in a fight?"

"I lost my job," Gus said. His almond-shaped eyes sagged in the dim light. "Instead of part owning this place, which was supposed to happen by now, I don't even work here."

"Terrence fired you?"

"That's right," Gus said. He took a hit off his drink. The deejay slid over to old Run-DMC, "My Adidas," and a few people sitting at tables crossed themselves and pointed to heaven. Gus took Soraya's hand and guided her over to the table that he favored, away from the staircase and all the noise. He sat down across from her and rubbed his chin. His hair was pushed back and messy. He kept shaking his head, like he'd seen something that surprised and scared him.

"Tell me what happened," Soraya said. She wanted to put his head in her lap, make it all better, but she knew that he'd get pissed if she acted motherly.

"We went out to his car and he told me it was over. He gave me a couple thousand in cash and a handshake. Didn't say why, just that he's going in another direction with this place, and since he already pushed me out of the hotel side, he figured he'd just set me free. He's still got a bad taste in his mouth from what went down last spring. I guess he needed to kick me to get clean."

"So what are you still doing here?" Soraya asked. "Fuck this place. We should walk right out." She moved to stand up, but Gus put up his hands. Stay.

"I don't have anywhere else to go," Gus said. His voice was low and it sounded to Soraya like he'd said that a few too many times to himself. But it was true. Even after Terrence Cheng had relieved him of his duties at the Official Hotel, Gus had lived in a room there. Now that Terrence had fired him, he really didn't have anyplace to be. He was instantly homeless.

Soraya glanced away from him. She had a lot of work to do at school, with finals coming up. She also had to declare her major and deal with how she wanted to sculpt her time so she could get the absolute most out of her Barnard education. She ran her fingers along the edge of the table, kept her eyes down. She loved Gus and didn't want him to see that she didn't need this kind of aggravation right now.

"You can stay up in my dorm room with me," she said.

"No," Gus said. "I know that you need to work and get that degree. I don't want to be a burden on you."

He finished his tequila and caught a waiter's eye, smiled, tapped his glass, and then made a gesture at Soraya—one for her, too. "Anyway, the staff is treating me real nice 'cause they know it's my last night in this place, for real. So stay with me, baby, and let's get fucked up."

"Gus . . ." Soraya could only shake her head. But Gus didn't seem to see.

"Just do this for me for tonight."

Drinks appeared in front of both of them and Soraya didn't try to tell him that he shouldn't be drinking. Not him, not with his history.

3 They were hard-core Texans, but neither wore a cowboy hat. They were both more than six feet tall and looked like they carried well over two hundred pounds. Franklin Novak ushered them into his private office. They sat down slowly across from him in the leather bucket chairs Franklin had been meaning to replace for the last five or nine years.

"I'm Ed Wallingford and this is Tom Stowe," the younger one said. "Our friends down at Wackenhut said you had several good years with them before you came back up north."

"They took care of me when I needed some help," Franklin said.

"You were kicked out of the NYPD for killing your partner," Ed Wallingford said.

Franklin didn't move. He watched the two men. He hadn't killed Billy Navarro. Soraya, Billy's daughter, knew that for the truth that it was. His son, Felix, knew it, too. He didn't care what anyone else thought. He felt for the men because they were grieving. But his past was his past. He had no need to explain it to anyone.

"What can I do for you?" Franklin asked.

"You know our situation," Ed said.

"I do."

"We need your help," Ed said. He stared at Franklin and Franklin took his time looking back at him. Ed's eyes were black. His hair was white and dense as a just picked boll of cotton. He wore a thick wedding ring made of white gold. He had on khakis and a blue blazer, and his shirt was as white as his hair.

Franklin glanced once at Tom Stowe, who was admiring the Beretta 687 Silver Pigeon II shotgun that Franklin had hung on the wall. It looked like Tom Stowe might not speak at all. He was only slightly older. Except for a wine red turtleneck sweater, he was dressed just like Ed Wallingford. Both men had deep creases in their weathered skin. Neither had much in the way of lips.

"I am sorry about your wives," Franklin said.

"We're going to be angry for a good while before we're sorry," Stowe said suddenly. He didn't smile.

"As I said, the way we heard about you was through our friends at Wackenhut," Ed said. "We called them first. They told us that for what we want, it'd be better to come to you."

"What do you want?" Franklin asked.

"We want them dead."

"Whoever killed your wives, you mean." Franklin said.

The Texas men met this statement with silence. Franklin tapped at the inlet between his nose and lips with his pointer finger. Jenny loved to trace this space. She said that it was called the philtrum, that it was one of the places where the soul lived. He doubted that, but he had been more aware of it recently since he'd been smiling with some regularity. He didn't smile now.

"I can find them or him. But I won't kill them," Franklin said.

"Let's leave off that part of the conversation. Let's just have you bring them in. Then we'll see. That fair?"

Franklin nodded.

"That's quite a picture," Ed said, nodding up at the framed Cookie Monster drawing that Lisa Gennardi had made, which hung behind Franklin's desk.

"Thanks. A family friend did it."

Franklin felt the words roll a little bit. He loved that idea, of family friends. Of course he didn't really have any.

"There's not a reason on God's earth why those two women were killed," Ed said. "Whatever it was, it had nothing to do with us."

"No one threatened you before this occurred?" Franklin said.

"It was their twice-yearly theater, dinner, and shopping trip. They were sisters, Maude and C. J. We'd have gone with them except we hate that sort of horseshit. We're oilmen. We don't have enemies. We have oil wells."

"So you don't know why this happened," Franklin said.

"Was a punk kid, I'd say. Thought he'd rob them and got scared. Made a mess of them. We can't say more than that. Don't know more."

"Well, I'll have more questions for you and you'll have to say more. There's paperwork, too," Franklin said.

"You can reach us here." Ed slipped his hand into his breast pocket and came out with a pamphlet, which he pushed across the desk to Franklin. The pamphlet was a small black-and-white thing, which advertised Dykeman's Cross, a duck-hunting and wild game preserve up in New Hampshire. An elite sort of place, where Dick Cheney might go for the weekend when security codes went up to red.

"We'll be resting up there till this is handled," Ed said. "We don't like the city. You got a question, come up there to ask it. We see you're not afraid of a shotgun. You come up there, shoot with us."

"I'd like that," Franklin said.

Tom craned his neck forward, as if he were about to say something. But he must've thought better of it because the line below his nose where his lips should've been didn't move.

Ed said, "We won't bury our wives till this thing is done. We know it's wrong. But we can't let those good women go into the ground until whoever killed them is found and put to justice."

"I'll do what I can."

Tom Stowe stood up, and Ed Wallingford followed his example. It occurred to Franklin, as they said their good-byes, that though Ed had done the talking, Tom was running the show, and one way or another, Tom would probably get to the man who killed their wives. He'd get to the man before Franklin did or after, but no matter—he'd get to him. And he'd kill him.

"You still with that girl reporter?" Franklin asked.

He walked rapidly down West Fifty-seventh Street with Felix toward the offices of AMC, Apple Management Company, where Stuart Apple was waiting.

Stuart Apple owned and ran the Sutherland with his son, Simon, and nephew, Morris. Franklin had called him after the Texans left his office. Apple had said he was aware of Franklin and was more than willing to cooperate. In fact, he was eager to talk.

Franklin figured this would be a good time to bring Felix in. Gennardi and Philip were out canvassing, seeing what their contacts in the street had to say about the case. Felix was scheduled to see Soraya later that night.

"You hear me?" Franklin asked. He jostled his son. They were both fast walkers. They were big men who moved with their heads down, as if their bodies were pushing against strong winds. Felix had adopted Franklin's habit of wearing suits that had no color beyond dark, and white shirts. He wore no tie, though, and he had on black boots. His father wore a battered pair of black standard issue Mephistos. Whereas Franklin was bald and hatless, Felix wore his battered white cowboy hat over his tangled hair. If people stared at the pair, the Novaks didn't notice.

"No, I'd have to say that's just about over," Felix said.

"You okay?"

"Me?" Felix looked up, his eyebrows suddenly arched. "Of course. I didn't love her or anything." And then he looked away.

Franklin laughed. "Course not," he said.

"Right, course not," Felix said. "So I got the part about the Texans from Gennardi. But I don't understand about Stuart Apple. He owns the hotel. So what?"

"So the police are in the hotel now, mucking things up and generally screwing the Apples' operation. We don't behave that way. I told Stuart Apple about our clients and he said, 'Terrific, however I can be of service, just let me know.' He wants the thing solved, and quick. And he wants to make sure it has nothing to do with the Sutherland."

"Does it?"

"Who knows?" Franklin said. "The Texans are right to be baffled. What kind of dingdong kills two old ladies in an elevator for their jewelry and their purses?"

"Somebody who's crazy?"

"Oh, that's the other thing. We have to be nice to the Apples. They have the tape from the elevator. The police are looking at it. Now we get to look at it, too."

"Well, that's really kind of them."

"Maybe for you nice means just keeping your mouth shut," Franklin said.

They turned right and arrived at a short building on West Fifty-sixth, half a block east of Sixth Avenue, next to the Parker Meridien. It was nothing—an office building of twelve floors plus a lobby, where an undersized doorman with a cap that had a silver apple on it sat behind a wooden desk that looked like it was ready to snap under the weight of his bag of sunflower seeds.

The floor directory said that Apple Management was on the fourth floor, which it shared with two therapists and a computer consultation service. The rest of the building was filled with small businesses: chiropractors, dentists, CPAs, a PR firm that represented musicians and chorus girls.

In the elevator Felix said, "You sure they own the hotel?" Franklin put his pointer finger to his lips. Then he whispered, "And a whole lot more than that."

Felix worked his jaw. The elevator smelled of age and camphor and wet wool. That same smell, mixed with steam heat, followed them down the green-and-brown corridor and into the waiting room for Apple Management. They were greeted by a woman with a nameplate on her desk, Joanne Gordimer.

"I'm sorry for the delay, but the Apples have requested that you wait for just a few minutes before going in," Joanne Gordimer said.

"No problem at all," Franklin said, and smiled at her. She was a short, heavyset woman in a black suit with an overlarge double-breasted jacket that covered her girth. The room was warm, and there were no windows. She pointed to a couch that looked like it had grown out of the carpet.

"Please be seated. We have magazines," she said.

"Great," Franklin said. "Thanks."

Joanne Gordimer disappeared behind a door with a rippled glass pane. Franklin smiled, picked up a copy of *Smithsonian* magazine from 1998.

"What the hell?" Felix whispered once they'd sat down. "This is how you solve a murder case?"

"Yep," Franklin said. He stretched out on the couch, made the thing wheeze a bit. "Article in here on the history of steam engines."

Felix got up and paced the little waiting room. There was no sound from anywhere. Franklin watched his son. He figured that Stuart Apple must be down a corridor, behind another door. Or perhaps he had a separate entrance and was not yet in the building. The most likely scenario was that he was on the phone with his lawyer, tending to his insurance.

"It's stupid to wait like this," Felix said suddenly. He stood in the middle of the room, stared down at his father.

"Take it easy," Franklin said. "Even these minutes have meaning. Think about them, about what we're doing."

"I don't—"

"Shut up," Franklin said in a different voice. "With your sister's case, I let you do some things your way. I couldn't think straight, either, with all that came up out of that. This time it's different. This time you learn what it means to investigate."

"What's it mean?"

"It means knowing when to be patient and when to act. It means understanding why someone might make you wait."

"Stupid to wait."

"Say it again and you're gone," Franklin said. "Investigating means knowing that every single word you say might be heard, that every time you turn, someone knows. I don't need you this time. Fuck around some more and you can head out the door."

Felix stood for another ten seconds, and then he turned and sat down on the couch with his father.

"Fine. What do the minutes mean?"

"I'm not sure."

"Well, wake me when you figure it out," Felix said. He closed his eyes and put his feet up on the coffee table.

Franklin watched the light from below the glass-paned door begin to dance. Joanne Gordimer came back into the room. She smiled and ducked her head slightly so that she appeared apologetic.

"Gentlemen? The Apples will see you now," she said.

She opened a different glass door than the one she'd come from behind. Felix and Franklin followed Joanne Gordimer down at least thirty feet of corridor. She stepped aside, and they entered a room that contained two men and no windows. This room smelled different, too, of lunch. The remains of tuna sandwiches in wax paper and bags of chips were visible in a wire garbage can.

"We are so sorry to have kept you waiting," Stuart Apple said.

"Don't think about it," Franklin said. He smiled at Stuart Apple, who stood behind a wooden desk with papers spread out over it, along with the napkins from lunch. Stuart was a small man and he was in suit pants and a white shirt, no tie. His sleeves were rolled up, exposing white, nearly hairless arms that resembled his face, devoid of expression and pale. His eyes were light brown, and so was his hair. He looked like he made it a point to avoid sunlight. He had a face, Franklin saw, that was made to be forgotten.

"No, really, it was . . . it was so stupid of us," the younger man said. "I'm Simon Apple."

Franklin watched Simon Apple smile at Felix. Simon wore a simple blue suit with a French blue shirt, dark blue tie. His hair was long and was carelessly tucked behind his ears. He had gleaming black eyes, like a ferret, but his face was open, with a broad nose and thick lips. He didn't look very bright, Franklin thought, and he probably got laid a lot and fooled himself into believing it was because of his charm.

They shook hands all around, and then Felix and Franklin sat down in two cheap white vinyl chairs with no arms. Franklin looked across at Stuart, who sat in a leather swivel chair. His son sat, too, slightly behind and to the left of his father, on a metal folding chair that he must have dragged out of a closet for the occasion.

"We're sorry about what happened," Simon Apple said. "We understand that you're working for the husbands of the women who were killed."

Franklin said nothing. Felix stared around the room and Franklin followed his son's gaze. Some framed photos of men shaking hands in front of construction sites. Bookshelves that were heavy with real estate trust papers. Franklin took it in. He thought how amusing it was that all this plus a lot of buildings made a man and his family worth far north of a billion dollars.

"That's right," Franklin said. For a moment he wondered whether one of their employees had killed somebody and they were covering it up. Franklin doubted it. They wouldn't stay this rich by helping people.

"We want to share everything we know with you. The faster this is solved, the better for us, of course," Simon said.

"Right again," Franklin said. "What can you tell us?"

"We have some tape of what occurred."

"Here?" Felix asked.

"This tape is news to me," Franklin said. Felix looked quickly at his father, barely masking his surprise.

"We'll show you what we have," Stuart said. In a slightly louder voice he called, "Joanne."

The woman who let them in appeared with a four-inch black-and-white TV, which she'd attached to a VCR. She set this apparatus on the desk and bent over to plug it into the wall.

"High-tech," Felix said.

Franklin watched Simon stare at his son. Simon looked older, twenty-five or so.

Joanne pulled out a tape and stuck it in the VCR. A tiny, grainy image of an elevator was suddenly visible. The sound of the elevator filled the room—it was incredibly loud. The two women stepped in. Only the tops of their heads and their shoulders were visible. But their breathing was easy to hear, as well as their comments. A man followed them in. He kept his back to the camera. Black hair, about six foot. Thin. They listened to the conversation, which was far louder and clearer than the picture.

They listened to the man discuss that he had instructions to make it sloppy.

"These are my instructions," the man said.

"Service type," Franklin said. "He understands that while he takes orders, they usually don't."

The man suddenly swept around and sprayed the camera. It was impossible to see his face in the movement. He didn't show it.

"Adept," Franklin said.

"'The first time I do this,' he said," Felix said.

The sound continued after the picture blacked out. Only one of the women had time to scream, and there was no way of telling which one. They listened to the noise of the women hitting the floor, of the grunts as the killer removed their wallets, their necklaces and rings and earrings. Heavy breathing filled the tape, and they could hear the doors open. The sound of footsteps disappearing.

"Not an athlete," Franklin said.

"One odd thing I'm sure the police will tell you," Stuart said. "He knew that was the laundry floor. That was planned."

"Of course," Felix muttered.

Stuart said, "He even spent some time there, wiping away the blood. He was quite meticulous."

"The bit about it being sloppy, then—you think it goes against his inclinations," Franklin said. "But we're already assuming he was hired."

"Yes," Stuart said. "Unless he was getting his instructions from God."

"He knew everything about that elevator," Franklin said.

"One ride would have told him all he needed to know," Simon said. "Though we're not, of course, against interrogating our employees. The police are doing some of that now."

"They've seen this?" Felix asked. Franklin watched his son play dumb. The kid made his mouth into an *O*.

"Of course. The police have a copy, and we're in negotiations now over how to release what we have to the press."

"That's up to you?" Felix asked.

"We own the cameras," Simon said.

"Isn't it state's evidence?"

"You recommend we hand it over?" Simon asked.

"We don't recommend anything," Franklin said, cutting in. "You're not our client."

"We'd like to change that," Stuart said. His voice was a whisper. Franklin thought the man used about as much energy as a penlight. No one spoke.

"You'd like this solved as quickly as possible," Franklin said. "But we already have a client. You understand that. However, if you'd like to aid us in some way, we're open, of course."

Stuart said, "The police aren't going to get far with our staff. We don't believe the problem lies there. It was some kind of robbery gone bad. A guy up from the South, looking to make a big score."

"The South?" Franklin asked.

Simon laughed. "My father thinks anywhere that's not Manhattan is full of undesirables. That's why we've spent forty years limiting ourselves to property on this island," Simon said. "He believes that if you go below Philadelphia, the whole country's nothing but a giant swamp."

"It's been a good strategy," Franklin said.

"Thank you," Stuart said. "Let's hope my son recognizes praise when it's set in front of him." Stuart turned slightly and raised an eyebrow at his son.

Simon frowned then, in a manner that approached a scowl, and scratched his neck with his nails. Franklin nodded, smiled at Felix.

"'The first time,' he said," Felix repeated. "He's going to do this again."

"We want to help," Stuart said. "That's all. Perhaps your people would like to stay up at the Sutherland. Observe things from there. In case whoever did this is planning to hit the Sutherland again."

Felix looked quickly at his father. Franklin seemed to be considering the idea.

"We've got a free presidential suite right now because of what's happened. Please do whatever you like with it," Stuart said. "Of course you can continue to count on us to help you in any way possible. In the meantime, accept a token of our respect." Stuart turned and looked at his son.

Simon opened an envelope quickly and removed a pair of tickets, which he held across to Franklin, who accepted them.

"Knicks tickets?" Franklin said.

"You can't beat those seats," Simon said.

Franklin held the tickets in his open palm. He watched Stuart Apple. Franklin thought that, save for his slight movements, his quarter-inch head turns and breathing, and the fact that his eyes were half open, he could've been asleep.

"We're all in agreement here," Franklin said, "that you're aiding us in the investigation. That's all."

"We understand completely that you are not employed by us," Stuart said. "There is no partisanship or self-interest here. We only want to catch this murderer and do whatever we can to alleviate suffering. Putting your operatives up at our hotel is the least we can do. Enjoy the tickets. We can't be in public just now in any case. More than anything, we don't want this to occur a second time, not at the Sutherland, not at any of our properties."

"People tell me that for the Knicks, this is finally the year of the rebuild," Franklin said, and as he stood up, he slipped the tickets into the breast pocket of his coat.

"Yeah," Simon said. "It looks like this could be the year before the year when it all comes together."

Felix and Franklin exited onto the street. They walked downtown, toward the office.

Franklin said, "Guy's worth over a billion in solid Manhattan real estate, he's eating tuna on wheat with lettuce off a piece of wax paper. No tomato, 'cause it's an extra forty cents."

"That's class," Felix said. "Isn't it?"

"No," Franklin said. "That's crazy. Even me, I spring for the tomato."

"And that tape, what a joke."

"What's a joke is how many other tapes they've got. And that's the one they show us."

"I don't get it."

"They got the lobby, the laundry, the stairway. They're hiding stuff, but you can bet doughnuts and coffee the cops got all that shit. And they know. . . ." Franklin went quiet.

"What?"

"That the cops aren't going to figure it out. I better have Gennardi talk to Eitel Vasquez. Nineteenth Precinct Homicide was never my thing. But Gennardi has connections there."

"Funny how Stuart and Simon linked up the way the guy said, 'The first time,' with all of Apple properties," Felix said. "They got a little ahead of themselves there."

"Maybe," Franklin said. "Or maybe that's just the way they see the world, in terms of their properties."

Franklin suddenly walked slower. He didn't feel like he understood the thing yet, but he didn't find it mystifying, either. He figured it'd be done in a week.

Felix said, "I'll go get Soraya."

"Yeah," Franklin said. "The two of you up at the Sutherland makes a lot of sense. You can watch the staff, and as far as anybody's concerned, you're guests. You should appeal to the side of her that'd like to stay in a high-class hotel. Actually, why don't you take her to the game? I'm going to make some calls, and then I need to see Philip and Gennardi. I had to cancel a homemade chicken potpie dinner with my friend to make time to get those two up to speed."

"When are you going to introduce me to the lucky lady?"

"When I put a ring on her finger," Franklin said.

"Good idea. Women like it when you keep them locked up till you're ready to marry them."

"Jesus," Franklin said. "You're getting like Gennardi."

"I hear he hasn't exactly been home every night lately."

"What's that supposed to mean?" Franklin asked, fast.

"Ask him. You think it's weird they offered us a room at the hotel?"

"I dunno," Franklin said. "It was after Simon got all aggravated and started scratching himself. Remember that; it's his tell. That's when he gives something up to cover himself. I think Stuart's just trying to keep us where he can see us. He's a nervous type. Anyway, put yourself at the game, and if somebody looks ready to answer a question, ask one.

You'll be sitting in the Apple seats and people are going to think you're high rollers. Afterward, go to the Sutherland and check in. But if the killer's a repeater and this thing has anything at all to do with the Apples, you'll be known as connected to them from the moment the old guy at the gate rips your ticket and gives you the stub."

4

Soraya said, "What if I don't want to?"

"I guess I haven't pitched it right," Felix said. "Let's get in there first."

Felix palmed the stubs and looked around. The bowels of Madison Square Garden were cold, and around them thousands of people streamed up the escalators. The crowd was muted, though, with most of the noise coming from the few couples on dates. The Knicks were having yet another terrible season, and coming to a game was nothing more than showing hope for the future.

Felix looked at the tickets again, went over to an old usher, and showed them to him. The man glanced at them and snapped to attention.

"This way, please," he said. The old man led them to an orange door with no marking. Felix felt suspicious, but the man was easily seventy. Plus who would be after him and Soraya? Felix couldn't think of anybody.

They went through the door and up a staircase into a small lounge with a group of round tables. Important people sat with their hangers-on at the tables, eating good-looking hero sandwiches and drinking beer. There were plasma monitors attached to each wall. Otherwise the room was nothing more than painted cinder blocks and no windows.

"You can stay here until the game begins," the man said.

"VIP lounge," Soraya said, without pleasure. She sat down and looked away from the film directors and movie stars with too much free time. There were also half a dozen extremely tall former pros in green crocodile shoes and suits with half a dozen buttons. Several of the men gave Soraya a smile, but she didn't respond. They ignored Felix. The monitors focused on the Knicks City Dancers.

"Look, our instructions are to check into the Sutherland tonight," Felix said, low.

"That's pretty fast," Soraya said.

"Soraya," Felix said. Then he stopped. He felt confused. Why should they fight? It was a job; she'd already signed on. What was the problem? He scratched at his neck and thought about Simon Apple. The way he'd glared at his father and scratched himself.

An older man in a turtleneck and brown suit suddenly materialized in front of their table. He was with his wife, who was in her sixties. She wore a black fur coat and her hair was dyed to a high black shine. She smiled down at Felix.

"You two here on the Apples' dime?" the older man asked.

"How'd you know that?" Felix asked. He straightened, pulled away from the table. He wasn't carrying his Para-Ordnance .45, so he spread his hands out over the table and got ready to flip it. Soraya smirked at him. Her message was simple. Relax.

"You were led to their table," the man said. He wheezed slightly, like the couch cushions in the Apples' musty waiting room.

"We're guests at the Sutherland," Soraya said.

"This is their table. You must be quite important guests."

"We've been treated very well," Felix said, warming to his role. "But there was an awful lot of trouble there last night and we were woken up. We complained about it, the deskman was apologetic, and here we are."

"Have you met the Apples?" the man asked.

"In passing. Stuart's quite nice."

"We see him here less and less. It's always his son now, with a different woman every time. I remember when Stuart came to the games with his brother, Max," the man said.

"That was what, twenty years ago? In the dictionary under *quiet* and *bitter,* they had pictures of Max."

"That doesn't make an iota of sense," his wife said suddenly.

"Where's Max now?" Soraya asked.

"He died back in '83," the woman said. "Boating accident out on the Sound. The mother went soon after. That made Stuart Apple one very rich man."

"Only problem is Morris," the man said. "In the dictionary under *dumb* and *young—*"

"It was a senseless and stupid comment once," his wife said. "Twice, I ought to take you out and shoot you."

"Who is Morris?" Soraya asked.

"Max's son. He inherited half of everything. Now Stuart has to run all family decisions by his nephew," the man said. He looked around before he spoke again. "Make sure you get a bag of popcorn before you go. It isn't good, but it gives you something to do with your hands while the Knicks lose."

A bell rang suddenly at a few minutes before seven-thirty. No one moved quickly, but everyone stood up. A couple of security guards opened a set of doors on the opposite side of the room and they were ushered into the walkway just above the first tier of seats. The shock of going from a small room to a cavernous space the size of a town was great, and even Soraya let out some breath as she stared around the arena.

They quickly found their seats, in the second row right behind the Knicks' bench. They sat down and watched the players finish shooting around and jog back to the bench. As the players came closer, they remained huge, and Felix and Soraya involuntarily flinched.

"They're twice as big as the Columbia team," Soraya said.

"You got that right," Felix said. "I met Simon, Stuart's son, earlier today. But I didn't hear a word about a Morris or a Max."

"Why would he mention a brother who's long dead?" Soraya asked. "I've heard about Simon, though."

"What?"

"Playboy," Soraya said, as if, by employing that antiquated term, she answered everything. "Two sisters from Texas are murdered in a hotel and we're talking about the owners like they're interesting. It doesn't make sense. Why would anybody want to draw that kind of notoriety to their own hotel? It'd be an employee who would do a thing like that. Unless the husbands hired somebody?"

Felix glanced once at her, then shook his head.

"What's the matter with you and Franklin? You're not open to all possibilities?"

"What's the matter with *you* is the question," Felix muttered. They glared at each other. Felix had taken a bucket of popcorn from the VIP room as instructed. He ate a few mouthfuls. Shut up and wait, he thought. Franklin Novak, lesson one. He watched the Knicks City Dancers go through some routines. He figured that if he and Lanie broke up, maybe he'd ask one of them out. But would they have much to talk about . . . ? He reminded himself that he liked a smart girl. He glared at Soraya and thought, But not too smart.

Soraya took her black hair out of its ponytail. She crossed her legs, turned to Felix, and her black eyes flashed. She was searching. Felix tried to hold her stare. God, she was beautiful.

"Terrence Cheng fired Gus," Soraya said. "It's put me in a crap mood."

"I'm sorry," Felix said, though he'd never really had a warm feeling or much sympathy for Gus, even after he'd helped take down Lem Dawes.

"And he was drinking last night because he was upset."

Soraya flashed her eyes at Felix again. "I shouldn't be telling you this. You don't give a shit about him."

"No, baby—" Felix stopped abruptly. He had no business calling Soraya baby.

"I'm sorry," Felix said. "I don't want you to be upset. But I said that you and I would show up at the Sutherland later. I already agreed to it. We're only undercover inasmuch as that's necessary. So it'd be good if we looked rich, but we're really just doing surveillance."

Felix shook his head at himself. Why couldn't he be more patient?

"You don't understand what relationships are," Soraya said. She sighed.

"I never claimed to," Felix said. "What with you always telling me I'm immature, how could I?"

They didn't speak for a minute, and Soraya took the bucket of popcorn. She held a few kernels in her palm and pulled them into her mouth with the tip of her tongue. Felix watched.

"You say you talked to the Apples this morning?" Soraya asked.

"Yeah. They need help, but they're not the client. They don't want their hotels to go down the toilet because of the murder."

Soraya chewed popcorn and Felix watched her consider her options. They didn't really need her for the case, but it'd be a lot easier to move around the Sutherland and not look like a detective with Soraya there to deflect attention. Plus she had a natural gift for investigation. The Miami Heat were announced to a solid round of boos.

"This could be good," Soraya said. "I just thought of something I could do that'd help Gus."

"Great," Felix said. "Go ahead and make it personal. Can you believe these seats?"

But Soraya didn't seem to notice at all. She was always like that, Felix thought. Never wowed by the city. It kind of bugged him. But then, he was never impressed with anything when he was with Lanie. And that probably bugged *her.*

The arena went dark and fireworks played on the video monitor that hung from the middle of the ceiling like an oversized chandelier. There was one particularly loud explosion on-screen, a strobe light effect, and then the announcer cut in: *"Ladies and gentlemen, please welcome your New York Knicks."*

And then Felix didn't think about the case anymore. He did have to wonder, though, as the players slapped hands and ran onto the court, why the hell he kept doubting himself in front of Soraya.

Franklin sat with Philip Moyo at his table at Zitto's, in the back. It was nearly ten and they were waiting for their dinners. Richard, their waiter, had taken their order without speaking once. It was one of his quiet nights. Franklin finished the glass of Bushmills on the rocks he'd gotten at the bar.

"Where the hell is Gennardi?" Franklin asked.

Philip shrugged. He sipped a glass of Barolo. Franklin frowned and neither man spoke. Franklin watched the entrance. After a minute Gennardi came in through the double doors. At nearly six-four and three hundred pounds, he was a great slab of a man, in a black suit and dark blue shirt. He was graying around the temples. Though he knew how to hit a man, he was no enforcer. Franklin preferred to do the hitting.

Gennardi slipped off his coat and handed it to the coat check girl, and then he stopped at the bar to talk to Karen. He lingered with her. Karen laughed. She was past forty, but she managed to look pretty good, even in a white shirt and black bow tie, with her red hair pinned up. She listened to Gennardi and then nodded at him with sympathy.

"He doesn't know we're waiting back here?" Franklin asked.

"He knows," Philip said.

Slowly Gennardi made his way to the table. He took the seat across from Franklin.

"Sorry I'm late," he said.

"Skip it," Franklin said. "We've been discussing the clients. We already discarded the idea that they had their wives killed. If they were going to do that, one, they'd need a motive, and two, they'd have done the job in Texas and avoided any chance of federal charges."

"So we've got nothing yet," Philip Moyo said.

"Look," Franklin said. "I'd like this thing closed within four or five days; otherwise it'll string out forever. What'd you guys learn on the street?"

Richard the waiter came and poured Gennardi a glass of the Barolo. Gennardi took a long sip.

"I love how you think we're going to bring you anything that's *street* on these Texas lady murders," Gennardi said. "Like I'm so down that the dealers on Stanton Street know my middle name."

"You have a middle name?" Philip asked. "Who knew? Mine is Adwoa."

"That's nice," Gennardi said. "Adwoa."

"His is Lucien," Franklin said. "Enough. I got Felix and Soraya checking into the Sutherland in a couple of hours. They'll watch, but it's not going to do much—it's not an undercover thing. Staff saw that killer, you can bet. And our clients want that guy dead. We deliver the killer to the police. Get paid, that's the end of it. Now let's backtrack. Is there anything you're hearing on the street?"

"The street," Philip said, and smiled. "It's all Dominicans in the laundry room up at the Sutherland. They're not really up to talking to us is what we learned."

Richard came to the table then. He delivered two steaks for Franklin and Gennardi, pasta al di mare for Philip. Suddenly the table was filled with food, with side dishes of broccoli and potatoes. Richard took the empty bottle of Barolo away and opened a bottle of good Brunello. He delivered fresh glasses and poured wine for each man. Then he disappeared without saying a word.

"So who kills two old women in an elevator?" Franklin asked.

"Either a nut or somebody who got paid to do it, and a nut couldn't loiter in the lobby of the Sutherland Hotel," Gennardi said. He cut a piece of steak, but then he didn't eat it. Instead he leaned back in his chair. He found his wineglass and drank long, again.

"Who would hire a killer if not the husbands?" Franklin asked.

5 "No bags, sir?" a porter asked Felix once he and Soraya arrived at the Sutherland.

"They'll be here tomorrow," Felix said. He eyed a police car that idled a few yards from the Sutherland's dark-wood-and-brass doors.

The porter nodded once. He was a short young man with brooding eyes and a potbelly. If he looked them over, Felix was sure it was only to gauge whether he'd be tipped. And Felix doubted whether the porter could tell, because in his sleek black suit and cowboy hat, Felix no longer looked like he was from out of town, but he didn't look like a true city type, either.

Of course, this couldn't be said of Soraya. They'd stopped off at Soraya's dorm after the game and she'd put on a lot of black clothes and a pair of very tall boots she'd borrowed from her friend Edwige Jamison. She looked rich.

And now here they were, without bags, checking into the presidential suite at the Sutherland. They stood in front of the night deskman, who ran Felix's credit card. He was bald and was about Felix's size. Felix could hear his breathing. The man looked like he had given up trying to sleep during the day years ago and now just didn't sleep at all.

"It's a nice room?" Felix asked.

"The best suite we have, sir," the deskman said. He nodded to himself and kept working on signing them in, as if he were performing surgery and needed to use complete concentration.

"Good," Felix said. And Soraya raised an eyebrow at him. The lobby looked like it should be quiet, but there was noise coming from one side, glasses tinkling and some music, what sounded like a piano. Soraya motioned toward a black glass doorway set on the north side of the lobby.

"That's a bar?" Felix asked.

"The Lido, sir. It's open for a few more hours if you'd like a drink before seeing your room?"

"No, we're beat. But it's a cool bar?"

"Young people seem to favor it. If you'll just sign here, sir."

The deskman held out a slip that explained that though they were comped in full, they were responsible for any damages. Felix signed. He said, "I guess you had some trouble here last night."

"We did. An awful thing," the deskman said. "But we're back to normal this evening. We pride ourselves on that."

"On taking killings in stride," Felix said. But his tone was meant to convey that if this was the case, it was fine with him.

"On doing all we can to keep our guests happy. At all costs. Enjoy your stay. And please call me with any concerns or problems. My name is Alexei."

"Alexei," Felix said. "Thank you."

They went to the elevator bank. One elevator was discreetly cordoned off with a yellow velvet rope and a small sign that said Under Repair. That was it. Twenty-four hours after the crime had been committed and it seemed to Felix that police presence was down to nothing save the police car out front and the requisite plainclothes cops lurking who knew where.

The only people in the lobby were Alexei the deskman, the doorman, and a couple who'd suddenly appeared in the glass doorway and were kissing under the relatively bright lights of the lobby. The deskman watched the couple for a moment and then picked up a phone.

Felix and Soraya stepped into the elevator. The ceiling was a flat pane of glass. Someone would have to know, then, where the camera was positioned, unless they covered the whole ceiling with spray paint.

They didn't speak to each other while they looked. Instead they made eye contact, nodded. Felix thought about how it had been when they were looking for his sister's killer. He was never able to hide his thoughts from Soraya, even when he tried. Felix swept his arm around and pantomimed stabbing the space where another passenger might be. He did this once and looked at Soraya.

The killings would have been a terrible mess. At that close range the murderer, whether he was under orders or not, was a psychopath. He would have had to consider proximity to the victim and ultimately decided that he was able to stand it.

The corridor of the penthouse floor was all cream-colored paint and white moldings, with worn baby blue carpet.

"That close and he couldn't flinch," Felix said.

"Professionally trained," Soraya said.

"Or he'd just been waiting to get his for a long time," Felix said.

They found penthouse C, and Felix passed the magnetic card through the reader on the door. The door swept open. They walked in and Soraya immediately went and sat on one of the two pink couches that faced each other in the middle of the living room. She slipped off her boots and put her feet up on the square white table in front of her. She stretched out and sighed. Felix hadn't made it five feet past the door. He looked at the big rectangular room. The ceiling was double height—twenty feet at least—and there were painted gray clouds that began at the tops of the walls and crept up into a clear blue sky that was dimly lit above their heads.

Soraya said, "Pull those curtains closed, would you? The light's going be hellish in here at noon."

Felix looked and saw thick gray curtains that were pulled back to reveal a dark view of Central Park. The room smelled very slightly of lemon and the several vases of fresh-cut flowers that were arranged on end tables scattered about the space. It was the most beautiful room he'd ever seen.

Soraya reached forward and took a copy of that day's *Spectator* from the arranged fan of newspapers and magazines that were on the coffee table. Then she yawned.

"You see a phone anywhere?" Soraya asked. "Let's call down and get some drinks and sandwiches. I hear this place has a pretty good chicken club."

"What the hell, you act like you were raised in this room. Fucking Eloise at the Ritz or whatever," Felix said.

"The Plaza."

"What?"

"Eloise at the Plaza."

Felix shook his head and sat down on the couch opposite Soraya. She leaned back and stretched, thrust her chest forward. She blinked at him and she looked like some kind of royalty. The princess of Puerto Rico. Her beauty kind of bugged him suddenly, and he looked away, reddened at his sudden anger.

She said, "Take it easy. Anyway, it's more like the opposite—Gus and I visit a lot of places like this for Terrence. Or . . . we did. He's coming over here in an hour or so."

"Who said he could do that?" Felix asked.

"Lose the snappy tone, would you? People are going to watch us no matter what we do. Especially the staff."

"We need to keep quiet, though—we're surveillance, and we're not supposed to make a lot of noise."

"I thought we were bait," Soraya said.

"I suppose we could be. But that's secondary."

Felix picked up a remote control and toyed with it. Behind Soraya a dim light grew in a large bedroom that was behind French doors.

He looked again at Soraya. God, was she ever beautiful. Man, was her beauty a pain in the ass.

Felix figured he'd sleep on the couch or they could sleep
in the bed, toes to heads. He didn't want to sleep in the bed
with her like brother and sister—no way. Last thing in the
world he needed was to have one of the nightmares that had
plagued him since he'd come to the city and wake up clinging
to Soraya, with her prying him off and his humiliating boner
popping up between them. Nope, sleeping toe to head
wouldn't do, either. He'd sleep on the couch. Shit, maybe
he'd sleep in the closet. Have her lock him in there.

Soraya asked, "Where'd they stay, anyway, these sisters?"

"A little room on the eleventh floor. They shared a bed.
Apparently they were cheap that way."

"Can we get in there?"

"We should be able to, yeah," Felix said. His cell phone
beeped once and he took the call.

"Yeah," Felix said. "We're in. We'll get some room service. Cash in the safe, right. I get it. What? No, they led in the
third by ten, and then they got blown out in the fourth quarter and lost by twelve, like always."

He flipped his phone closed and dropped it in his jacket
pocket.

"Franklin," he said. "We'll have luggage delivered here
tomorrow. And the Apples are going to leave us some cash
to put in the safe. So if the motive was nothing but robbery,
we'll have that attention. They're going to give us a list of
employees who were fired in the last two years, too. And if
we see Gennardi and Philip in the building, we don't know
them."

"They're being very helpful, these Apples," Soraya said.

"You notice much activity here? Sixty percent of the place
checked out this morning after they turned on *New York One*.
Rich people don't want to sleep near danger."

Soraya's Blackberry went off. She read the screen.

"That's Gus. He's not coming up here after all. Says he's too beat." She frowned.

"That's too bad," Felix said.

"Shut up. He'll be here tomorrow night, that's for sure."

Felix stood up and went over to a white marble bar. He got behind it and opened the freezer, took out some ice. He found a little bottle of J&B scotch and opened it. He hated how her sad frown was connected to Gus.

"What kind of sandwich do you want?" Soraya called out.

"Roast beef," Felix said. "And a cold can of Budweiser."

Felix took a warm slug from the bottle of scotch before pouring the rest over ice.

Someone knocked on the door. Felix and Soraya looked at each other. Felix eased his .45 out of his shoulder holster and went and stood at one side of the door.

Soraya slipped off the couch. She grabbed a thin vase, upended its water and flowers into the sink, and hefted the cylinder as if it were a baton. She positioned herself on the other side of the door and nodded once.

Felix said, "Yes?"

A voice said, "Midnight snack, compliments of Simon Apple."

Felix shrugged, stood square in the doorway, and opened the door. A porter stood there with a rolling service table. It was covered with food. He rolled it up to a table that was set off at the far end of the big room and began to set up the meal. Soraya had already turned back to the sink, where she was rearranging the flowers.

It took the man a few minutes to set things up. There was a bottle of Mersault, sparkling water, and several small dishes, each covered with a glass top.

"This was nice of Simon," Felix said.

"Yes, sir," the porter said. He quickly tossed a salad and slipped the tongs into a drawer in the service table.

"Just leave the table outside the door when you're done," the porter said. He glanced around the room once before he left but never caught Felix's eye.

"I wanted roast beef," Felix said. "But I'll settle for steak medallions. This Apple is certainly trying to make us feel at home."

"Or maybe he treats everyone this way," Soraya said. "I'll have to ask Edwige. She knows him. She told me he's been fighting with his cousin for years. Simon's the smooth one and Morris is the sad fat boy. That's how it's always been."

"We need to meet Morris soon. And I could ask Lanie what she knows about their history," Felix said.

"I don't see why. If we want to hear the sort of rumors that belong in the *Spectator*, we can make them up ourselves."

"Thanks for that."

"The fact that you're still with her amazes me."

"But I'm not with her," Felix said as he speared an asparagus tip. "I'm staying right here with you."

Soraya smiled. "Well, then. Back in business. At least this time the killer hasn't picked off anybody we know."

"It *is* a nice change," Felix said. And then he suddenly shook his head. He cupped his ear and pointed at the serving table. Soraya said, "Of course. Nothing we say to each other means anything, anyway. You know that."

"It's all meaningless flirtation."

"That's right," Soraya said. She watched as Felix slowly worked over the serving table. She ate the salad. There were blood oranges, and she loved them. But if there was a recording device, he couldn't find it.

He said, "It's unfortunate that Simon's mentioned to the staff that we're here."

"We don't know that he said we're doing surveillance."

"Are we?" Felix asked. "On whom? It seems to me that

my father and I went to see someone and they brought us close just to keep us out of the way."

He shook his head. The room was huge. A recording device could be anywhere.

"That isn't cool," Soraya said.

"No," Felix said. He circled Soraya slowly. She hadn't moved. "It's not cool at all."

6 "So how ya been?" Franklin said. He was trying to smile at Eitel Vasquez, who was really Gennardi's friend. He was also trying to ignore the fact that Eitel had been on the Internal Affairs committee that had barred him from returning to the NYPD a dozen years earlier.

It was four o'clock on Friday afternoon and they were in a booth in the back of the White Fox Lounge, on East Ninety-ninth and Madison, just north of the Nineteenth Precinct's jurisdiction. For whatever reason, the owner of the Fox was partial to show tunes, so they were listening to *Oklahoma,* just a little loud.

Eitel was on one side of the booth, facing the door, and Franklin and Gennardi were on the other, facing him.

"I was fine till this stupid double murder. National attention. I hate that." Vasquez shook his head. He was a thin man with sunken eyes and black hair that he wore blown out and parted in the middle in a style that hadn't garnered praise since 1981. He wore a black raincoat and a brown suit, a gray shirt, and a tie that was black as a subway tunnel.

"Have to report to the commissioner?" Gennardi asked.

"Every six hours," Eitel said, and checked his watch. Then he looked squarely at Franklin. "Who's your client?" he asked.

"Come on," Franklin said. "Don't be like that."

Eitel shrugged. "I'm about ready to piss on those Apples for all the help they've given us on this," he said. "I know you talked to them yesterday, 'cause we're watching their office. You and your kid. So if they're your client, then I'm walking out of here now."

Franklin shook his head no.

"Okay," Eitel said. "I can deduce the rest. Maybe we can help each other? But I'm on a fucking egg timer, so let's snap it up. This was an inside thing with a disgruntled employee. The Apples treat their people like shit, like the Ciprianis with their restaurants. Union busting, no workman's comp, whatever sleaze they can get away with. These motherfuckers, they don't exactly share the profits. So what I hear is this was a laundry room guy who was laid off and went back in, liked the idea of making a mess on the sheets, but then he couldn't wait, got himself off in the elevator."

"So if you know that much, why not go get him?" Gennardi asked.

"Maybe I'm doing that right now," Eitel said, nodded to himself. He was drinking a tequila sunrise. The bathroom door opened behind them and the sudden glow turned his cloudy drink the color of a streetlight.

"But you need us," Franklin said. "Why?"

"Why'd the Apples come to you?" Eitel asked.

"I went to them," Franklin said. "They offered us a hotel suite for surveillance. I said yes. So I got my son and Soraya Navarro on the inside."

"I've heard of those two plenty already," Eitel muttered. "I'm talking to you on the off chance I'm wrong. I'm sure I'm not, but if there's some other angle on this thing, you're going to tell me about it. If the killer came up from Texas or if it was a pro thing where somebody's trying to ruin the Apples, you'll follow that angle. I can't afford not to share with you."

"That's sweet of you," Gennardi said.

"Look," Eitel said. "I'm not Mike fucking Sharpman, looking to double-cross you scumbags and then get my ass railed right off the force. You think nobody but IA watched that nitwit go down? I'm clean, and I run a good homicide unit. But last time I checked, the two bodies in the morgue were rich and white, and the newspapers are saying they bled like

a couple of Texas longhorns, so I got to cover every base."
Eitel slid his card across the table.

He said, "You get something, you call me."

"What do we get in return?" Franklin asked.

"I'm grateful and I don't impede you. And when I nab the former employee who seems like the dumb ass who did this thing, you can ask him whether the ladies had any last words and give those to your client with the compliments of the NYPD."

"On the tape he says he's taking orders, that he's going to hit the Sutherland again," Franklin said.

"Yeah. I got my fingers crossed he had delusions of grandeur. But if this was contract and it's all about the hotel, you're going to untangle that web of info quicker than me. So do it."

Eitel finished his drink. He stood up and shook hands with Gennardi, looked away from Franklin, and walked out.

"It was good to see him again," Franklin said.

"Got any smart ideas on how to make him a little easier to handle?" Gennardi asked.

"A nice column in the *Spectator* ought to do it," Franklin said. "He'll be more helpful if he's a little puffed up. Remind me to talk to my ex–father-in-law. Starling likes to do that kind of favor."

"That's not gonna move Vasquez."

"Maybe not. But it's always nice to have Starling Furst on our side. And the quickest way to do that is to get him to think I owe him."

"He'll bother you about your ex-wife," Gennardi said.

"That's okay. Think of it as my way of checking up on her."

There was a soft rap on the suite door at seven on Friday night. Soraya rushed to open it. She'd put on a tiny bit of perfume, the Guerlain she liked, that only accented her natural scent.

Felix sat on a sky blue velvet lounge chair in the bedroom. He flipped channels on the television, but Soraya knew that was bullshit—he had the true country boy's lack of patience with TV.

She'd turned down the lights in the suite and had the stereo going, tuned to WBLS, evening jams, and the sweet sounds and the low light in the beautiful room were melting her a little. She wished Felix wasn't hanging around. She'd been in class all afternoon and now she was up for some sex.

"Hi, baby," Gus said.

Soraya reached out to him without saying anything, pulled him into the suite. She kissed him and burrowed her head into his shoulder. He was in a good black suit and a black turtleneck, but he didn't smell right. It wasn't alcohol or even his own perspiration she was smelling. It was something else. She didn't know what. She didn't like it and her desire left her.

"You okay?" she whispered as she led him to the couch. "Felix is here."

"Course I'm okay," he snapped. "Why do you always have to ask me that?"

She'd been holding his hand and she felt a tremor go through her, as if anger were coursing through him like current. She liked that even less and let his hand go.

"Hey, man," Felix yelled from the bedroom, twenty feet away. "We can order up some food if you want something."

"He has to be here?" Gus asked, and he sounded pleading.

"Part of the deal, baby," Soraya said. She moved closer to Gus. She kissed his cheek.

"Cold out?" she asked.

"Not really," Gus said. "Why?"

"Your cheek."

"I'm stressed, baby. I never lost a job before," he said. "I looked around all day but . . . I didn't hear about anything I liked."

They heard Felix's heavy stride as he came into the room.

"You have a place to stay?" Soraya asked.

"Not really, baby," Gus said. He looked around the suite. "These Apples may be dirtbags, but they sure know how to maintain a piece of property."

Gus went to the kitchen area. He opened the fridge, pulled out a tiny bottle of Stoli. Soraya watched him without saying anything. She was more amazed at the speed of his transformation than anything else. She'd never seen him drink vodka before, and now he finished off the little bottle like it was as routine for him as his espresso craving or his chocolate craving. She frowned at Gus and hoped Felix wasn't watching.

"The carpet in the lobby was all worn down, though," Gus said. "Me and Terrence would never allow that."

"Heard you got fired," Felix said. He was flipping through a copy of *Vanity Fair*, turning the glossy pages fast.

"You heard right," Gus said.

"Felix, you're supposed to read that, not just look at the pictures," Soraya said.

"We didn't have books like this back on my mom's farm. Heck, I never saw one till I got to New York."

"It's not a book." Soraya glared at Felix. She said, "Gus, why'd you call the Apples dirtbags?"

"I don't know the old guy . . . what's his name, Stuart? The reclusive billionaire type. I know his kid, though, Simon. And the cousin, Morris. Those boys think they know something about hotels. They come into the Official with a bunch of their friends and order beluga and Cristal like they're part of Def Jam and they still believe they're going to make money off Mariah Carey or some equally wrong-headed bullshit. Then they leave a mess." Gus paused. He'd finished the little bottle of vodka and helped himself to another one. He took the first and dropped it into a white garbage can. "That's how you know you're dealing with dirt-bags. They leave a mess."

"Thanks," Felix said. "That was an invaluable lesson. You ought to be a detective."

"I'm thinking about it," Gus said. He pursed his lips. He was holding the bottle tight in one hand.

Nobody spoke. Felix checked his phone. He looked at his nails. He waited.

"I suppose if I said I heard them talking about taking the business away from Stuart, you wouldn't believe me, huh?" Gus said.

"Baby, you don't have to offer us information to hang here. I want you to be with me no matter what," Soraya said.

"Who is 'them'?" Felix asked.

Gus looked exasperated. "The cousins, Morris and Simon."

"I wouldn't believe you, no."

Soraya and Felix glared at each other. The room was quiet, and only dim lamps from the bedroom and the night sky illuminated the living room.

Felix said, "You two spend some quality time together. I'm going to take a walk."

He stood up. He'd hung his suit coat in the closet by the door and he went to get it. Gus watched him.

"I helped you once," Gus said. "I gave you Lem Dawes when you couldn't get him yourself. Now maybe you could be open, give *me* some help."

Felix turned, looked at Soraya.

"I *am* giving you some help," Felix said. "I'm leaving."

Felix slipped on his coat and took his cowboy hat from the shelf in the closet, placed it on his head.

Soraya thought he'd look back at her, but he went out the door without turning around. The door drifted closed behind him and then locked.

Gus said, "It's true what I said about the Apples. I wouldn't just offer information if I didn't know it firsthand."

"It doesn't matter. I believe you," Soraya said. "You sure you need to be doing all this drinking, baby?"

"Say what?" Gus asked.

"Nothing." She looked away from him toward the window. She blotted at her eyes, which were glistening with tears.

Gus finished the second bottle and went looking for a third. "I can't believe fucking Terrence. It's for real. I checked with everybody. He doesn't want me anywhere near his places anymore. I don't have any money. I'm in a fucking mess and I got to dig myself out, fast."

"I'm sorry, baby," Soraya said.

"Don't be sorry," Gus said. "I don't want your sympathy. I'll get a job in a day or so."

Soraya looked away. She didn't say that sympathy wasn't what she meant.

The elevator doors opened in the lobby and Felix stepped out. He wanted to see Lanie. In the lobby the noise from the Lido Bar was loud, since half a dozen patrons had leaked out of the place and taken over a group of lounge chairs far from the door. They were Eurotrash and young, Felix's age. Several women and a few men, tall lanky types who looked like they never slept and never worked. Never did anything but drink champagne and bottled water and gossip about sex. Felix felt like he hated them, and then he felt so tired he didn't even bother to ask himself why.

He moved toward the door and saw Gennardi and Philip at the desk. He went over to the deskman, intentionally coming close to Philip, who went stiff at the sense of somebody so close.

"Hey, Alexei, where can I get a cab?" Felix asked.

"See the doorman, sir," Alexei said.

"Cabs drive on the street, so that's where you find them," Philip said.

"Thanks, man. I'm from out of town, so I wouldn't know that."

"I guessed as much just from looking at you," Philip said.

Felix walked away. He was impressed. He could probably come up to Gennardi and Philip with a monkey on his head and his shoes on fire and if they were undercover, they wouldn't blink, acknowledge him, or put him out.

Out on the street, he started walking downtown and called Lanie. He thought about what made Philip and Gennardi so professional and knew that it was that they didn't take things personally. It was work and they did it because it was good work. But they didn't get like him, all attitudinal and pissed off at everybody. He wished . . . but then Lanie picked up.

"I'm at Au Bar," she said, "with the richies. Come get me, baby. They're tearing me to pieces." Before she ended the call, he could hear her laughter.

"You're always out with the richies," he said. But he knew he was only talking to the street. Au Bar was on East Fifty-eighth Street. He kept his pace, kept walking. Tried to imagine what being a real professional detective would feel like. Maybe he wouldn't feel so knotted up and knit-browed all the time.

"What else?" Gennardi said.

"I already talked to the police," the deskman said.

Philip let out a huge yawn, and he made a noise while he did it, a kind of rumble.

"I'd praise Allah fourteen times a day," Philip said, "if I never had to hear that line again."

"You guys aren't going away, are you?" Alexei asked. They'd been there for half an hour before Felix stopped by and fifteen minutes since.

"You see the face of every man and woman who walks by," Philip said. "We watched you. Because this is one of the top five hotels in New York, you make eighty-five thousand dollars a year, and you're perhaps one of the top five most valuable people in this hotel because you see all, and you track all, and you tell nothing. You've been here eleven years and never had a problem that went beyond kicking out the occasional drug-addled hooker. Now there's this. It's a problem. You saw the women. We know that. You spoke to them. You saw the man. Tell us about it. And if you use the police line again, my friend here is going to call your boss and end your career."

Gennardi smiled. He enjoyed it when Philip did the talking. His English had a heavy tint from growing up in Zimbabwe, and his voice, with its deep bass resonance, coming from such a tall, thin man with such big eyes, tended to scare the hell out of nervous types. But Alexei only frowned. His thin lips sagged and dragged his face down.

"I told the police I saw a man, thin like you, but not as tall. White man. But I never saw his face. I believe he made sure I only saw his back."

"Who did see his face?" Philip asked.

Alexei looked down at the computer monitor embedded on his side of the desk.

"There was a maid who said she saw him running. She recognized him. But she quit. Maybe the women in laundry up on three know where to find her. They don't speak English, though. And they'll be afraid of you. The police already scared them pretty good."

"Thanks," Philip said. "How do we get there?"

Alexei showed them to a staircase behind him and went back to the desk. The lobby was increasingly loud because of the people from the bar.

"He only showed his back because Alexei would recognize his face," Gennardi said as they started to climb the stairs. "Otherwise he'd just act natural, be forgettable."

"Right," Philip said.

They opened the door on three and the sound of two dozen industrial-size Morain washers hit them. There were six women and two men ironing sheets and a few others working the machines. The floor was a vast space, unbroken by anything except white columns. The ground was concrete and dirty, and the walls were gray. There were no windows. The workers were too busy to even look up.

"This air is like home," Philip yelled.

They walked around for a moment. Only three elevators opened onto the floor, two freight elevators and one passenger elevator.

"Vasquez was right," Gennardi said. "He had to know the place inside and out. Only one elevator gets him here."

They frowned at each other and nodded. The whole job had been arranged from the inside. They went over to a woman who was slowly ironing a coral-colored pillowcase with white piping.

"Pardon me," Gennardi said in Spanish. "Do you know of a maid who was working here two nights ago when the man—"

The woman walked away. She didn't even shake her head. She'd left the iron on the pillowcase, and steam and smoke immediately started to billow up from it. Nobody came near Gennardi and Philip or the burning pillowcase.

"We might as well go," Gennardi said. "Everybody here already got warned or got paid. They're a lot more scared of whoever did the deal than they are of us."

Carefully Philip stood the heavy iron on its end before the blackened pillowcase set the ironing board on fire.

"How's the case?" Lanie asked.

"I can't tell you that," Felix said.

They stood in a corner of Au Bar with drinks in their hands. Music was playing, an old Nana Mouskouri number the Europeans liked. All around them men in dark turtlenecks and crocodile shoes sat with women in overpriced blue jeans and colored silk shirts. Lanie drank water from a squirt bottle that she quickly placed back in her bag. Then she sipped at her martini.

"What are you doing in here, anyway?" Felix asked.

"It's a freelance job. I'm going undercover as an American so I can see if I get treated badly by all the Eurotrash in here and then I'll report on it for *New York Undercover.*"

"But you're friends with half the people in here," Felix said.

"I know." Lanie laughed. "It isn't really working."

"Half the time I don't understand what the fuck you're talking about," Felix said. He signaled the bartender and didn't notice the guy's glare. He ordered a Budweiser, and when they didn't have that, he told the guy to bring him two fingers of Yukon Jack in a water glass. The bartender nodded, went to the other end of the bar to find the bottle, and told some other patrons about it. They looked over and burst out laughing. The bartender stopped what he was doing and lit a cigarette. One of the patrons tried to whistle the theme from *Gunsmoke.*

"This is great," Lanie said. "They're really laughing at you, which proves my point. Thanks. Now let's time how long it takes for you to get served. Then I've got to go to a party. But that won't be fun for you."

"What party?"

"I can't tell you that," Lanie said, in a voice that mimicked his own.

Felix looked down at the dark wooden bar. All around him he could hear young people chattering in languages he didn't understand.

"I don't think we should go out anymore," Felix said.

When he looked to his right, he saw that Lanie had drifted away. She wasn't even talking to anyone else. She was just looking around and keeping her distance from Felix. The bartender still hadn't brought him his drink.

"I'm going now. I'm leaving. Will you have your cell on later? I'll call you," Lanie said. But she was about eight feet away and she seemed to be floating about five feet above the ground.

"What's going on with you?" Felix asked. But Lanie was slipping on a short black coat. She wasn't going to explain. She left without kissing him, without looking back.

And it was only then that he realized there was no point in breaking up with her. They'd never said they were going out. So when he'd said that they shouldn't, just a few minutes before, she'd heard him perfectly well. She just didn't want to deal with it.

"Oh, hell," Felix said. He got up and caught a cab back to the Sutherland. When he opened the door to the suite, the doors to the bedroom were closed and the lights were out. It was still pretty early, but he took off his boots and his hat and lay down on the couch with his clothes on and tried to go to sleep. He hadn't known they weren't really going out. While he lay there, he admitted that all he was doing was arguing with his woman, just like the guys did in Smuggler's Notch back home, just like his father had with his mother. But apparently rules were different now. And there'd never been a single thing that was proprietary between him and Lanie.

He stood up and looked out at Central Park. He thought he missed her. And then he thought about Soraya, in there with Gus. So many things to dislike. The only thing that felt good was the soft Himalayan rug under his feet. He squatted and put his hands on it, and then he lay down on the rug, closed his eyes. He wondered if he was feeling yearning, if this was what it felt like to need someone to really love you for real.

"Hey," Soraya said. "It's okay."

Felix looked up from the floor. Soraya had her hand on his forehead. He said, "What is?"

"You. You were tossing around and yelling. You must've had some kind of nightmare, but I couldn't understand what you were saying."

He sat up and looked around. He said, "I'm fine. Where's Gus?"

"He had to go. He thinks there's some work at a club in Chelsea, so he went down there. I stayed. I wasn't sleeping when you came in." Soraya sighed. Then she whispered, "Gennardi called. He's sure it's an inside thing. We don't know if the guy was hired, but he knew this place real well. We have to learn more about these Apples."

"Tomorrow," Felix said.

"You going to sleep out here?" Soraya asked. She stood up, straightened. She was in a long white hotel bathrobe that covered her shape. Felix was only up on one elbow. He looked at her ankles. His only thought was that he'd never seen them before. He saw that they were slim, that her feet were small, the arches high. Her toenails were painted a dark color.

"Yeah," Felix said. "I'm beat."

"How's your girlfriend?"

"She's not my girlfriend," Felix said.

"Good night, then," Soraya said, and disappeared from

the room. "But if you're going to wake up in the middle of the night, you might as well sleep in the bedroom so I can put my hands on your head and shut you up."

"I'm not going to," Felix said. "That's just how I sleep, tossing around like that. It's no big deal."

"Yeah, right," Soraya said.

7 "Just the man I wanted to see," Starling Furst said. He stood in the doorway of the University Club and greeted Franklin Novak, who was also a few minutes early.

Starling said, "Tell me, have you spoken to Ellie lately? I recall that when she left here in June, you agreed to see each other again."

Franklin smiled. Starling Furst, his ex-wife's father, was still, still, after all these years, meddling in his daughter's life. He'd said that he hated everyone in his family, that he couldn't give two pigeon shits about any of them. But here he was, trying to repair his daughter's marriage, which had gone down in a hail of bullets and adultery nearly thirteen years earlier. Charming, Franklin thought. Charming, and fat fucking chance. Part of him suddenly wanted to tell Starling that he thought he'd finally been able to fall in love again, but he knew he would sound ridiculous. And he didn't want that. But he didn't want his first wife, either. Not anymore. So he said nothing.

"You don't want to talk about Ellie," Starling said.

"Not now. Tell me about the Apples," Franklin said. They walked through the busy lobby and went and stood in front of the tall windows that looked out over Fifth Avenue, where tourists were already gathering for their Saturday morning strolls. The men didn't look at each other. From behind, they only looked like two businessmen. One older and regal, tall, in a thin suit that hung on him and seemed to shudder from the slightest wind, like dark gauze. The other was shorter and completely bald, in a suit that was creased in all the wrong places. He looked like a bodyguard or some sort of protector, clearly a minion, taking orders.

"Stuart Apple," Starling said. "He owns plenty of good

property. He's eccentric. I can't say I know him. He doesn't see many people—makes me look like a social gadfly by comparison."

"Butterfly?" Franklin asked.

"No," Starling said. "I know what I said. I meant gadfly."

"So you annoy more people than he does? I suppose that makes sense. Did he kill his brother?" Franklin asked. "I've been reading old newspapers. I know that Max Apple died in a boating accident off Oyster Bay, but the water's not so wild there. I'm wondering if you heard a different story."

"No one ever thought that Stuart killed his brother," Starling said. "The money came from their father. A Jew like you. Stephan Applebaum. He owned some buildings around Sutton Place—one of them still houses La Cote Basque. And he was quite a gentleman. I recall him coming to real estate meetings in the fifties. He had a gold-tipped cane and I can probably recall the three or four times he ever said anything. He knew how to buy a property and hold it. But of course, his sons were much more aggressive. They turned a good small business into an overlarge corporation. But both brothers were eccentric."

"Like how?" Franklin asked. He'd turned and was watching the white men in suits who were drifting into the University Club. They were big men, mostly from out of town. Franklin had no opinion about them. He was just looking at their faces. None of them looked like the Texas husbands. Those old boys were tougher, with lines in their faces that said they'd spent good parts of their lives working outside. Suddenly Franklin felt terribly sorry for the husbands. He listened to Starling tell him the history of the Apple family. After a while a few items stood out, but Franklin wasn't ready to put them in order—not yet, anyway.

"I appreciate you giving me this information," Franklin said.

"Least I can do," Starling said.

Franklin said nothing.

"You saved my life. That's no small thing," Starling said.

Still Franklin didn't speak. After Starling had realized that he had sent his granddaughter toward her death, he'd tried to step in front of a bus. Franklin had saved him, yes, but he'd only saved him from himself. Franklin didn't think that counted for much.

"Listen, Ellie's running out of money. She may have to sell her farm. I want her to come back here. I think you could take care of her."

"She's a grown woman, Starling. And she left me more than thirteen years ago."

"Twelve and a half. I won't pursue this now. But I won't forget all you've done for my family." Starling clasped Franklin's shoulder and started to walk with him toward the elevator bank. Franklin checked his watch. Noon. He shook his head, thought, If he wants me to remarry his daughter, the least he could do is take me to lunch. But that would have been too much. Starling had a reputation to maintain.

"There is one thing," Franklin said.

"Yes?"

"A lieutenant in the Nineteenth Precinct, homicide division, name of Eitel Vasquez. He's looking at the Apple case and I need to buy him some extra time so he doesn't do anything stupid. A nice piece in the *Spectator* about him would be terrific."

Starling ground his teeth for a moment. Franklin knew from experience that this meant he saw an idea he liked.

Starling said, "I'll get that nice Lanie to do it. She's bored with the city hall beat. I'll give her this."

"She'll do perfectly. I was just going to suggest her," Franklin said.

"I know you were," Starling said. "Stuart Apple is above nothing. You ought to remember that. And you should give your ex-wife a call. I know she'd like to hear from you."

Starling Furst walked away from Franklin before he could respond. Franklin watched him go. He thought, You can count on a man who pulls strings to keep on pulling strings in order to keep himself vital and alive. And then he thought how angry the old man'd be when he told him there was no chance he'd go back to his first wife. No chance at all.

While Franklin waited for the elevator to his office, Jenny Hurly came up behind him. He knew it was her because he heard her heavy, slightly asthmatic breathing, and he smelled flowers he couldn't name. This was how he'd met her, waiting for the elevator. She worked on his floor, for a photographer named Ivan Bulgarov, though she was looking to quit.

"Guess who," she said as she came around him.

"Bulgarov have you running errands on Saturdays now?"

"No, I had a lunch date and I decided to come in here and take care of a few things. An interview, actually. I'm not going to be Ivan's assistant much longer."

In the elevator Franklin kissed Jenny softly.

She said, "What was that for?"

"I don't want to lose you," he said. "People who don't care about people who love them, they regret it forever."

"That's so sweet of you," Jenny said, and she kissed him again. "It's so sweet of you to realize that. But don't worry about me. It's your son you need to hang on to right now. I saw him in the hall earlier, waiting to see you. He looked like hell."

"Thanks, Jenny," Felix said. He wouldn't let her go, though the elevator doors had opened. "You should come and have dinner with me and him, maybe Soraya, too."

"You're ready for that?"

"I think so," Franklin said.

"I'll come by tonight."

"Good," Franklin said. "That sounds good."

Jenny went into Ivan Bulgarov's studio, and Franklin went down the hall and into his office. The only thing that was waiting for him there was a large cardboard box, which had been placed just inside the front door. It had arrived by messenger, and he imagined that Gennardi must've been there to receive it earlier in the day.

When he hefted it, it felt like it was filled with phone books. He opened it carefully with the knife on his Leatherman. With his other hand he covered his face entirely with a rounded sheet of rubber-backed lead that he kept expressly for opening packages. Once he was sure there was no sound, gas, or movement coming from within, he peered at the contents of the box. It was a leather gun case with *Smith & Wesson* emblazoned on the top. There was an envelope resting in the case. Inside the envelope was a note from Tom Stowe. It said, *Thought you'd like this. Ready to shoot some apples off the tree?*

He opened the case and stared down at the new 500 Smith & Wesson Magnum, the most powerful production revolver in the world. It was a satiny steel, utterly stainless, and perfectly clean. Worth at least a thousand dollars.

He hefted the gun. It was almost five pounds and about fifteen inches long. A five-shot revolver on an X frame with a Hogue rubber energy-absorbing grip. Even though the box said that the recoil was tamed with an effective muzzle compensator, he knew that it'd probably knock a weak man across a room and flat on his ass. He rummaged around in his desk and found a box of Hornady bullets. He slipped them in place. Then he took out the Raging Bull he kept in his shoulder holster and replaced it with the Magnum. The

Magnum was even bigger than the Bull, and it made his left side list down slightly, as if his center of gravity were skewed.

He pulled it out and aimed at his phone, dry-fired once. He wondered how much the Texas husbands already knew. And he knew he'd have to go and see them and ask them why they were thinking about the Apples. If they expected him to shoot someone, he at least wanted to know who that would be before he told them he wouldn't do it.

8

Felix waited for Soraya to finish dressing. They were headed down to the Lido, where Sean Lennon was going to play piano at midnight.

"How do I look?" Soraya asked. She came out of the bedroom wearing black high heels, shimmering black pants, and a silky peasant shirt.

"Rich," Felix said. "Now let's go."

"I ought to look rich. These are Sigerson Morrison heels. The pants and shirt are both handmade by Jane Mayle. I got all this stuff from Edwige. That's what you're going to wear?"

Felix looked down at his vintage cowboy suit. It was the color of soot, with piping that was now off-white. He had on hand-tooled cowboy boots that were scuffed at the heels and a black shirt with a spread collar.

He'd stuffed the black suit that Lanie'd gotten him into a laundry bag and shoved it in his duffel bag. He sort of suspected that he might've ruined it, but he didn't care. He said, "What's the matter with what I'm wearing?"

"Everything. You look like you walked off the set of *Coogan's Bluff.* I know that's your favorite movie, but that doesn't mean you have to dress in period costume. But it's too late to worry about it now. Here, I'll take it down a notch so we don't look so off when we're together."

When she went into the bedroom, she left the French doors open, but she didn't look back at Felix. She slipped off the black shirt and Felix watched her naked back. He could see her breasts sway as she moved, reflected in the mirror above the bed. And when he looked at her face, he could see that she was watching him. She didn't cover herself, but she stepped into the bathroom.

Soraya came out again, and now she wore a bone white

turtleneck sweater. Her hair was spread out against it and Felix thought about the image he'd just seen, about how he didn't feel like they were family. But he couldn't figure out how to say that. Instead he pulled in some air and looked away. She came up behind him.

"Don't I look nice?" she asked.

"Yes, you look nice," he said. "But you didn't tone it down like you said you would."

In the elevator Soraya said, "I'm tense. I think there's something the matter with Gus."

"No kidding," Felix said.

"Don't be an asshole, Felix. I'm serious."

"Sorry," Felix said. "But I've always thought there was something the matter with Gus."

Soraya frowned then and bit her lip.

She said, "I should be wearing more jewelry."

"Don't worry about it," Felix said. "There's nobody who wouldn't want to get close to you tonight. But remember, right now this is still a waiting game."

"I know. But I can almost feel how hungry they are, whoever they are. They want to make their next move."

"I know," Felix said. "I can feel it, too."

The door opened then. Felix went over to Alexei and asked him for five thousand dollars from their safe. The man went into another room, and in less than a minute he brought the cash back.

"Have a good evening, sir," Alexei said. He didn't blink. Felix watched him. No mention of how odd it was to deal with cash this way. No suggestion to keep it in a bank or in traveler's checks.

Felix and Soraya went across the lobby into the Lido. A host showed them to a booth. The bar shared the same cool blue color as the hotel, but here it was accented with ivory and black. A black piano stood on a small stage that was raised only a foot or so above the rest of the room. A pale yellow spotlight shone down on it.

The crowd was very young, as young as Soraya and Felix. A waitress in a thin black leotard came over and they ordered drinks, cold sake for Soraya, whiskey and beer for Felix. Occasional bursts of laughter from a group just in front of the piano punctuated the otherwise subdued atmosphere.

"Nobody here would rob us," Felix said. "This is a waste of time."

"Let's just hang out then, have a drink, see what we can see."

"Does Sean Lennon interest you?"

"Sure. He's a friend of Edwige, just like everyone else."

Sean Lennon suddenly came in, dressed in a white velour track suit. He went and sat at the piano. Several beautiful women followed him in. They stood near the door and made a show of being nervous. An older man asked them to put out their cigarettes and made some noise about smoking being illegal, but they ignored him and a waiter led him away.

Felix leaned his head against the cool velvet sofa and watched Sean Lennon toy with his piano. He sounded like he was about to break into song, but then he'd slump over, and no sound would come out save a sort of breathy cry. It was almost charming, Felix thought. But then, it was also almost boring.

"No, really, I am sorry," Felix said. "About Gus, I mean. I hope he's okay."

He suspected that it was something about the music, the lack of center in it, that made him see that there was no reason he shouldn't be nicer to Soraya. He reached out and touched her back where her sweater was scooped out and he could feel the heat of her bare skin. She looked away from the stage and focused on him.

"What about Lanie? What's going on with her?"

"Nothing good," Felix said. "I guess my friends back home would call us hook-up friends or something. We hook up when it's convenient. Less than that." He knew he sounded like he was trying to convince himself.

"You beer-goggle each other at 4 A.M.," Soraya said, and laughed. "Just like the country kids at school."

"No reason for you to be kind to me, is there?" Felix said.

But before Soraya could answer, Simon Apple came in through a small door that was next to the kitchen. Felix motioned to Soraya. Simon took a table by a far door and sat down. A woman followed him in. She seemed very young, perhaps as young as Soraya.

"The handsome one is Simon Apple," Felix said.

Then, from the same entrance, another young man came and sat down at the table. He was heavier than Simon and less attractive. He wore an expensive but poorly cut chocolate brown corduroy suit and a red-and-white-checked dress shirt that was rumpled. Simon looked as smooth as he had when Felix had seen him two mornings earlier. Tall and razor clean, in a simple black suit and white shirt. There was some family resemblance between the two young men, the same curly black hair, the same small features clustered around the middle of the face. On Simon, the whole thing worked. On the other man, everything was off. But it did look like he was trying.

"The other is Morris Apple," Felix whispered. "The cousin."

The two cousins began to talk while the woman watched Sean sing. It wasn't a big room, and the ceiling was low, and Sean Lennon seemed to be growing more comfortable. He sang in a whispery, high voice, accompanied by a drumbeat that played from a small machine. A few people seemed to watch Simon and Morris as they talked. But no one said anything. Felix wished he were closer than forty feet away. He watched their faces. Simon suddenly bared his teeth. He glared. Felix didn't recall him having done anything like that at their meeting.

"Not true!" Morris said, too loudly. His voice was a bit high, and Felix realized he was younger than he'd first appeared. He was probably only a year or two older than Felix. Twenty-three or twenty-four.

"Quiet," Simon barked at him.

"I think Morris went out with my friend Edwige," Soraya said. "I'm quite sure I've met him before."

The two cousins were really arguing now, and suddenly Morris stood up. His face had reddened and his hands were visibly shaking. Sean Lennon didn't pause. The women who were watching him were ignoring the Apples, too. Apparently Sean was working out a new arrangement of one of his father's songs. Short of gunfire or an anthrax scare, Sean Lennon evidently had no trouble holding a crowd's attention. Though he didn't act hungry for it.

"End of it," Morris seemed to say. He swept his glass and Simon's onto the floor, but instead of going out the way he'd come, he walked the length of the Lido toward the front door.

"If you can think of something to say to him, you ought to follow him and say it," Felix said. Soraya nodded. She stood up and glared at Felix. Then she went out first, ahead of Morris. Simon was standing now, touching the place where his pants had gotten wet with drink. He'd been watching his cousin go and then he caught Felix looking at him. He raised an eyebrow. Who was the girl? Felix shrugged. What girl? And then Sean Lennon suddenly finished his set. He stood up and said a few words to the women who had come up from the back of the room, but no one could hear him. Then the house music came up, which was fifties swing. This made everyone laugh. In the confusion Felix caught Simon's eye.

Simon was beckoning to him. Felix sighed and pushed his unfinished drink away. He stood up and made his way through the crowd.

Outside the Sutherland, Morris bumped into Soraya. She made this happen simply by observing his movements in the blackened window of a car and then stepping backward when he came forward.

"You're a friend of Edwige's," Morris said after he regained his balance. "I remember you."

"Yeah. We met at her house in Oyster Bay," Soraya said.

"Two summers ago. You got in an argument with Edwige's mother over how she treated the cooks."

"That's me."

Soraya looked uncertainly down Madison. There were plenty of cabs; she only needed to hail one. But she was waiting to see what Morris did. She was still fairly near him and she thought he smelled slightly of champagne and sushi. His clothes were all handmade and his wristwatch was enormous. An aesthete. A dilettante. A fop. She thought, I can handle this.

"I'm headed downtown," he said. "Let me give you a ride."

"Fine," Soraya said. She turned then and really smiled at him, the wide-breaking smile she used rarely that invariably softened people. Morris's eyes widened. A black BMW sedan pulled up to the curb and Morris ushered Soraya into the backseat. He sat down next to her and sighed deeply, brought his knee up to his face and frowned.

"Where to?" Morris asked.

"Well . . ." Soraya checked her watch. She waited another beat.

"Maybe you'd like to have a quick drink before heading home?"

"Sure, because you're a friend of Edwige's and all."

"We're not too close anymore, actually. John, take us to Suite 16."

Soraya looked out the window. Suite 16. Jeez—last year's hot spot, which was now filled with pro ballplayers and hookers. She'd expected something more relaxing for this grilling. The Water Club or Estate, at least. She'd even have been satisfied if he'd brought her all the way down to Sway.

"You were in a bit of a spat back there," she said.

"Nothing new," Morris said. His voice was high and tired, "Who was annoying you?"

They sped down Fifth. For a moment Morris said nothing. He checked his watch. A limited edition Breguet, Soraya noticed. Fifty thousand dollars at least.

"My cousin, actually. We've got some business together, and we can't agree on anything. He's hateful."

"What was tonight's problem?" Soraya asked. And then, rather than looking intently, she dropped her head back, closed her eyes, and breathed deep. She crossed and uncrossed her legs and for just a moment rubbed her knee against his. He'd want to do some talking.

"We had a murder back at the hotel a few days ago. You may've read about it. My uncle's upset. Now my cousin's upset. It's loads of fun when they act this way, believe me. I mean, we've got the kind of corporation that ought to run itself, and they do nothing but worry about it."

"So why should any of it bother you?" Soraya asked. "If it runs itself." She hadn't moved. She opened her mouth. Ran her tongue over her upper lip. Not like me at all, she thought.

"Oh, we just disagree about how to help the police," Morris was mumbling now. Soraya felt him come closer. They were driving through the park. It was an unnecessarily long route, and the trees made the night that surrounded them terribly dark.

"Who wouldn't help the police?" Soraya said. The driver put on some music. Sade. How cliché, Soraya thought.

"That's what I keep saying," Morris said. "I can't imagine what we have to hide. Faulty security? I mean, sure, we may be liable, but my father always said taking blame up front was what made you a man. Then again . . . But tell me about you. You're a fan of Sean's music, or do you just like the scene?"

"Oh, I was supposed to meet Edwige, but she never showed up."

"That's like her," Morris agreed. "She's a hard one to pin down."

She felt his hand on her shoulder, on her jaw. She opened her eyes then. She raised her shoulder once and then twisted away from him with a pivot of her hip. Whether he was aware of it or not, he'd given something up, and now he wanted something in return.

"Lord, I'm tired," she said, louder. "My boyfriend is going to beat my ass blue for being late like this. Maybe I ought to go home."

"Where might that be?" Morris asked. His voice was resigned. She knew he'd lost out like this before. She felt kind of bad. But it was late and Morris couldn't seem to stop staring at her. So she told him to take her to McBain, her dorm at Barnard. She couldn't see any reason to hide where she was living, and besides, she was tired. If he was going to find out who she was, he'd have done so already. And he hadn't.

"I'd love to see you again," Morris said. His voice was a little high and wheedling. He wasn't fat, really. Just awfully soft. Overcared for.

"Sure, that'd be great," she said. "I like to dance. We should go dancing. But now I've got that angry boyfriend to attend to."

She made a show of yawning as she got out of the car.

*　　*　　*

"Thanks for joining me," Simon said to Felix. "I was about to look like a prize ass."

"How could that be," Felix asked, "when you have such beautiful company?"

But the girl at the table, who Simon had introduced as Paola, didn't seem to hear. She took out a cigarette and lit it. She smoked and stared at a point over Felix's head.

"She's upset because Sean ignored her. Aren't you?" Simon asked.

Paola stood up suddenly and walked to the bar. She was very short, but she was painfully beautiful, like Penelope Cruz, but in a bad mood. Around them the music switched to a rumba. Several people got up and pushed their chairs away from them and waiters rushed to their tables to make sure that their drinks were not upset. They started dancing in an awkward circle.

"Sorry if I'm to blame for her leaving," Felix said.

"Paola? She's just angry because she wasn't the center of the conversation. Now, what's going on? You learn anything? My father's desperate to get this thing taken care of."

"Tell me," Felix said, "what was the problem over here?"

"Problem?" Simon asked. "No problem. Family business. Nature of the thing. Occasionally we disagree."

"That was your cousin who walked out?"

"Yes," Simon said. He paused. He frowned and scratched his neck with his nails. Felix nodded. And then he scratched his neck, too.

"The thing is," Simon said, when he got finished with his neck gouging, "my cousin is really nervous about this killing. He keeps saying that if it happens again, my father is going to fall apart."

"Doesn't that bother you, that he says that about your father?"

"Yes," Simon said. "He's such a scheming little fat boy, you know? You've got to wonder, when he says something like that, whether he's up to something."

Paola came back to the table then. She didn't sit, though. Instead she swayed between Felix and Simon, and she glared down at Simon. She grabbed up a bunch of Simon's thick hair and pulled his head backward so he was forced to look up at her.

She said, "I'm bored. Either we dance with my friends or we go fuck, and then we meet my friends later."

Simon stood up then, slowly. He grinned and said to Felix, "I guess I'll see you around."

And Felix watched Simon and Paola go over to the group of messy dancers and begin their air kisses and goodbyes. Felix sipped his scotch and watched them. He was alone at the table, but he didn't care. He got up and wandered into the Sutherland lobby, where it was quiet.

Alexei stood behind the desk. He watched Felix approach.

"Quiet night?" Felix asked.

"Just as it should be," Alexei said. "No problems at all."

In the elevator Felix began to text-message Soraya. He told himself he wasn't worried about her, not at all. He just wanted to make sure that she was okay. She wrote back: *Office A.M./info to share.* Good, Felix thought. He wiped at the sheen of cold sweat on his forehead. He fumbled with the credit card door key and prayed he'd get through the night without nightmares.

9 "It was an inside job," Gennardi said to Franklin. He and Philip Moyo were sitting with Franklin in the office, waiting for Felix and Soraya. It was Sunday morning. They were drinking coffee and eating thick slices of banana bread studded with almonds and white chocolate.

"The entire laundry room was handled," Gennardi said.

"They know the killer and they're afraid of him," Philip said.

"Seen this?" Franklin asked. He handed his new Magnum across his steel desk to Philip. "A present from the clients."

Philip whistled low. He slipped his Desert Eagle .44 from his shoulder holster and aimed both guns at the Cookie Monster picture that Gennardi's daughter, Lisa, had drawn for Franklin.

"Watch it," Gennardi said.

"For the first time since I came to work for you, yours is bigger than mine," Philip said. "I'll have to go shopping this afternoon."

"Mine was a present," Franklin said.

"You said that," Gennardi said. "Where'd you get this banana bread, anyway?"

"Jenny made it this morning. We got up early and baked together."

"And then you made love," Philip said. "You two're sweet."

"Can we talk about the case?" Gennardi said.

Franklin nodded at Philip. "Let's. It's no fun to see a big man cry."

"The way I see it," Gennardi said, "those two women were random targets. They got into that elevator at that time, and they got shanked. It's a very ugly, very stupid way to destroy a business."

"Some righteous mother or sister will call the police," Franklin said. "That'll be how we find the killer."

"Maybe," Philip said. "But this guy will kill again first."

"Because?" Franklin asked.

"Because he was fantastic at his work and because he enjoyed it," Gennardi said. "That's the thing that nobody counted on."

"He made the news," Philip said. "The whole thing went better than he could've hoped."

"What about the earpiece?" Franklin asked. "The fact that he was taking directions?"

The door buzzed. Felix and Soraya came in. It was ten-thirty. They were more than half an hour late.

"We don't know who gave him orders. Do we?" Franklin said.

Philip smiled. He shook his head.

"We've got some ideas," Soraya said. "You might want to let us talk first." She was wearing a black turtleneck and black pants. Franklin could smell her, the way her good smell overpowered the male odor of his office.

"If you'd been on time, we could've done it that way," Franklin said.

"We were up late, working," Felix said.

"In any case, I want to begin with my story because it's the oldest," Franklin said. Gennardi and Philip moved to the couch along a side wall. They splayed their legs out and looked sleepy. Franklin knew they had answers, but they'd be relaxed about it. They liked process, and they knew their story would come last.

Soraya and Felix took the leather bucket chairs that sat across from Franklin's desk.

"You sure you don't want to hear what we saw last night?" Felix asked.

"It's important," Soraya said. "We discussed it this morning."

Franklin gestured to Philip, who handed back the

Magnum. He slipped it into the drawer that already held his Raging Bull. He knew they'd sent him the Magnum so he'd shoot the killer with it. And if it came to that, he'd do it, but he didn't love the idea. Not like they thought he did, anyway. Everybody was shifting around, waiting for him to get going.

"I saw Starling yesterday," Franklin said. "Back in the fifties, there was a man called Stephan Applebaum, and he owned one building, eight stories of apartments on York Avenue, just off Sutton Place. And he was happy. No more growth. Around 1970 or so his two sons, Stuart and Max, took the building away from him. They were around thirty years old at the time. And they'd both been failures. They'd done their time out at Berkeley, tried to be rebels. But nothing worked. So they came back home and looked around. And they stole their daddy's building."

"How?" Soraya asked. "I don't get it."

"They declared him incompetent, but he was fine. He was a Holocaust victim and he was prone to seizures. The thing was settled out of court. These boys were ambitious. They took that building and leveraged it, kept the old man in an apartment on East Fifty-seventh Street near their office. Shit, maybe he's in their office now, locked up in a closet or something. He'd be about ninety-five. So these two young nuts, they don't get married or anything. They work insanely hard. Stuart bought a hotel, then another, and he got ahold of the Sutherland. Max bought commercial real estate. Very lucrative, not sexy at all. They both got married when they were in their late thirties, and around 1980 or so, out come two boys, Simon for Stuart and Morris for Max. Looks good for everybody. Then Max died."

"How?" Felix asked.

"It was a boating accident off Long Island," Philip said. "He had a speedboat, and he ran into a ferry. He sank."

"Accident?" Soraya asked.

"Let's say it was," Franklin said.

"Stuart Apple takes control of the whole operation," Felix said.

"Not exactly. There's Max's widow, Ina. And there's the son, Morris. Ina moves out to Arizona when Morris turns eighteen. Gives him the house. A year later she's dead, too. Accident with a golf cart."

"How much property are we talking about?" Soraya asked.

"Then? Half as much as now. They never sold a building. They behave just like Felix's grandfather, who never sells or gives away anything. He clued me in on all this. About twenty commercial buildings, seven or eight hotels. They got into parking lots, but that's a whole different racket, so they got out. They bought apartment buildings."

"So bring us up to now," Felix said.

"You're impatient," Franklin said. "It's a problem. Like the way you ate that bread. It's good, but you just shoved it down. You didn't taste it. But what about now? You fill us in."

"I did taste it," Felix said. "There were too many ingredients. It wasn't subtle. Not like my mother's, anyway. Okay. About the Apples. It's a warring family. What was quiet big money is now loud money, huge money. And were you to ask me, I'd say Simon Apple wants all of it. Now let's hear why." Felix turned to Soraya. Franklin nodded, watching his son.

Soraya said, "I took a ride with Morris Apple last night. His line to me is that he doesn't understand why Simon won't help the police. That's a big deal. Me and Felix, we were talking this morning and we think we do understand."

"This Simon, he gave the order," Philip said from the couch. But Franklin heard his careful voice. Philip was only making a suggestion, not a deduction.

Felix's foot began to jiggle. He said, "Simon's behaving

like his father did. He's going to sacrifice the Sutherland and wrest control of everything from his father. Then he's going to destroy his cousin, maybe kill him. Just like his father did his own brother." Felix leveled a gaze at his own father. He said, "He's just like his dad. And we need to stop him before he tries to prove it all over again."

No one spoke. Franklin opened a drawer, took out a *Romeo y Julieta* cigar. But then he eyed the last slice of banana bread and put it back. Jenny Hurly didn't like the cigar scent on his breath and his clothes.

Franklin jutted his chin at Gennardi and Philip. He said, "This stuff jibe with anything you two learned?"

"There are two or three different kinds of employees at the Sutherland," Philip said. "The mostly white ones who deal with the public, the accountants and management who are only there during the day, and then there's maintenance. That last group is a huge number of people. They know this killer and somebody got to them, scared them. They won't give him up. But we can say for sure that he knew the layout of the hotel, he knew the laundry room, and he knew people there. Otherwise he couldn't have pulled it off. I'm sure the police know that, too. Who whispered in his ear, said, 'Make it sloppy,' or whatever, that connection we don't have. Did it come from an Apple to a killer? Maybe. It's a messy connection, though. What's a murder do? Create upheaval, ruin an insurance rating, destroy a reputation. It's bad business, whoever's doing it. I don't buy it yet. We'd need to catch the killer and ask, simple as that."

Gennardi said, "On that score, Eitel Vasquez is probably much closer than us."

"So now we wait," Franklin said. "But there's two things you four should know. One, a question: Why'd the Apples act so friendly and give us a room? Why are they feeding us information like it's almost nap time and we're whining for milk and cookies? Two: I don't have good news for my clients. And I need good news for those old boys soon. So let's get it."

"You get through to any of the staff?" Gennardi asked Soraya.

Soraya said, "A maid asked me if I was a pop star from Brazil."

"What'd you say?" Franklin asked.

"I told her I was a Puerto Rican girl from the Bronx and she got annoyed and said Jenny already left the block. So now she thinks I'm hiding something."

"Live it up over there," Franklin said. "Let's stay wide for another day or so. I don't want to work the Apple angle unless we've actually got something. I want to stay open to the street, the staff. Don't forget that we're looking for exactly one killer. Not a conspiracy. Not a family tussle. We just need one guy."

"But you don't believe that," Felix said.

"It's not about believing. It's about the client," Franklin said. "You two get back there, throw some pillows on the floor, and tell the maids to pick them up. It's time you two drew some attention to yourselves and sped this thing up."

After Soraya and Felix left, Philip and Gennardi took back their seats.

"So?" Gennardi said.

"So? No joking now, how's Dianne?" Franklin asked. "When are me and Philip coming over for stuffed shells?"

Gennardi looked down.

"You checked into a hotel, didn't you?"

"The Sperling," Gennardi said. "It's a cheap Apple property."

Franklin picked up the last piece of banana bread and ate it. With his mouth full, he said, "I think I'm going to tell

Jenny Hurly I'm in love with her and maybe we ought to get married."

"Good for you," Philip said. "Thirteen years between marriages is legitimate. Not even your son could fault you. But you ought to introduce them, and soon."

After that, nobody spoke. Philip straightened his blazer. He'd taken to wearing a black turtleneck, a blue blazer, and charcoal slacks, and the clothes looked good on him. Like an updated Steve McQueen. Franklin doubted that he'd stay with the operation much longer—unless the job simply amused him when he wasn't busy with his more political work. He was definitely making better money elsewhere.

Philip fiddled with his shoulder holster, adjusted it. He said, "We know this isn't going to break wide at the Sutherland. There's a police car across the street twenty-four hours a day. He'll do it somewhere else next time, whoever he is."

"Why'd you think I let the kids stay over there?"

"But he'll kill again," Philip said. "I'm sure of it."

"Wouldn't you?" Franklin asked. "If you did such a bang-up job the first time?"

10

Soraya shut the water off and got out of the shower. The Sutherland bathroom was huge, all old-fashioned black-and-white tile, with brass fixtures and thick towels that hung from heated rails. Everything in the baskets was free, all the beauty products, the manicure sets, everything. She looked at her face for a moment in the heated mirror. She'd been thinking about Morris for the last few hours. She knew he was lonely. And he'd be angry at someone because of that loneliness. Though that wouldn't necessarily make him violent. Anyway, she had her own problems. She needed to see Gus. She needed to call her mother, too. But she needed to see Gus more.

She came out of the bathroom and stood in the living room, where Felix was reading the *Spectator.* It was five on Sunday afternoon, and they were waiting for the night to begin. On Franklin's suggestion they'd ordered champagne and oysters, and Soraya had invited some people over. They were doing nothing on surveillance, so they'd decided to switch to bait.

"Gus'll be here later and then we'll go eat somewhere," Soraya said. "But first Edwige will come over with Lu-Lu Searle and Agatha Erdrich. I told them to bring some boys."

"Great," Felix said. He had his feet up on the coffee table. He tossed the *Spectator* aside and picked up an old article in *Real Estate Week* about the Apples.

"It'd help if you had friends," Soraya said.

"I was just thinking that," Felix said.

Soraya frowned. She was wearing a massive white robe. A white towel was wrapped around her head.

Felix said, "You look nice." And then he hunched forward and grabbed a toothpick because clearly he hadn't meant to say anything.

"I'm wearing a towel, idiot."

"I meant you look . . . nice and clean."

"Your shirt is lighting up," Soraya said.

Felix looked down and saw that his breast pocket was pulsing yellow. He pulled his phone out and saw the caller's name, then dropped it back in his shirt so that the display faced his chest.

"Who is it?" Soraya asked.

"Lanie."

"Why don't you get it?"

"I don't know," Felix said.

The house phone rang then. Soraya answered. She and Felix were staring at each other.

"We need a little more time," Felix said.

"Tell them to wait in the bar. Half an hour, please," she said. She hung up the phone. "I need to get ready. Don't move, darling, don't do a thing." Soraya shook her head and walked out of the room.

Felix looked after her. He text-messaged Gennardi and Philip that the party was a go. Felix hunched over, gritted his teeth. He wanted action. Instead he was getting a cocktail party.

He closed his eyes for a few minutes then, tried to imagine the idea of patience. But all he could think of was the nightmares he'd had the night before. He had chased beautiful women on horses through the city. They'd disappeared down manholes that were suddenly rabbit holes. When he'd followed, he'd found caves full of strangers who kept apologizing, saying they were sorry they were such a disappointment to him. He hadn't known how to explain that it was his fault, too. But what was his fault, exactly? He opened his eyes. Time had passed and he'd been sleeping.

"Hello, bright young things!" Edwige said when she arrived. She was trailed by several young people who were all attractive and who immediately sprinkled themselves around the room like so much brightly colored, overpriced furniture. They seemed to have arrived with the champagne and the oysters—either that or they'd brought their own.

"If it isn't my favorite little crime fighter," Edwige said.

"Hi, Edwige," Felix said. She sat down on the arm of the sofa and began to talk very fast. Felix was fairly sure they'd only met once or twice before, but she was acting like they were old friends.

When he couldn't find the right thing to say, Edwige got exasperated. She suddenly kissed Felix hard on the lips and went into the kitchen.

A very serious looking French graduate student in a gray flannel suit arrived and said Edwige had called him. He'd brought a stainless-steel briefcase and he told them he was going to use a series of beakers to mix perfect Kir Royales. Then Edwige came and sat in Felix's lap. The whole room smelled of her scent, something handmade from Bendel's.

"I'm going to make a man out of you tonight," Edwige said.

"Are you sure you don't have me confused with someone else?" Felix asked. And Felix looked so forlorn and unable to be charming that finally Soraya had to tell Edwige to leave him alone.

"But he's so cute," Edwige said. "He's so little boy lost and won't say his last name to the police!"

"Man," Felix said, "this is some Sunday night." He knew his voice was foggy, croaking. Felix refused the Kir Royales, which flashed in everyone's hands like red sparklers. He called down to room service and asked for the cheapest beer they had.

"Fuck it, then," Edwige said. She was looking out at the park. "I'm going to get some real people over here."

"Won't they be nervous about this place's new reputation?" the graduate student asked. Felix eyed him. The student licked a finger and ran it over his right eyebrow when he thought nobody was watching.

"Getting iced in the elevator? No way," Edwige said. "They're into the macabre of it."

"Do you like things that scare you?" Felix asked. He looked around. Where the hell had Soraya gone?

Edwige began to dial and then looked over at Felix again. "Wait, you can't be flirting with me finally?"

Was he? He didn't think so. But she was oddly riveting. And she was beautiful. Felix said nothing. There had to be twenty-five people in the room.

"Forget it," she said. "Soraya wouldn't like it."

"What?" Felix said. "Where is she?"

"She's got her own boy problems," Edwige said. "I don't want to add to them." Then Edwige was on the phone again. "Hello, Wes? Bo? Either of you—you're invited to a marvelous party."

And then it was past one and there were forty people in the room. Then fifty. Felix couldn't believe that Lanie hadn't gotten wind of the event. And everyone joked about murdering each other in the elevators if they didn't get a drink, or a toot, or a yank in the bathroom. Felix thought it felt like movies he'd watched with his parents before they'd split up, of wild parties in the Roaring Twenties that went on for days. He felt so strange—he wondered if someone hadn't put something in his drink. And then Edwige was in his lap again. She was patiently telling him how little she liked him, how she wanted him to leave her alone.

"But I am," Felix said. "Aren't I?"

Felix saw Gus show up. They eyed each other warily. Gus came over to the couch and shook hands, and then he backed away.

"Now I'll keep you busy," Edwige said, and pulled Felix off the couch. They went to play spin the bottle with a bunch of Barnard students in a corner of the big room. They were all girls and suddenly Felix was the center—no matter where the bottle pointed, somebody kissed Felix. He took the last can of Bud that he'd gotten from room service out of the breast pocket of his jacket and finished it. He looked around for Soraya and Gus, but he couldn't find them anywhere. And he thought, I'm not being a very good detective. Then Edwige kissed him on the lips again, and he gave up all hope of thinking clearly.

"I said I wanted to talk to you, but you were too busy putting up a front," Gus said after he and Soraya had gotten into the bedroom and kicked out the grad student in gray flannel and an equally earnest young man in blue jeans and a sweater, with whom he'd been making out in the closet.

Soraya bit her lower lip. This new Gus whined at her more often than not. He never talked about magic, about dreams, or anything like that.

"What's the matter?" Soraya asked. She reached up to touch his cheek and he moved away. But not before she'd felt the coldness of his neck. She'd had two drinks hours earlier and was quite sober. As opposed to Felix, she thought, who was completely bombed. She hated to be worried about him, too. But it was apparent that he hadn't slept through the night in several days.

"I asked Simon Apple for work this afternoon," Gus said. "I said I could help out with the Lido and their other hotel bars. I told him I could get some magazine people in to do photo shoots, which would be free publicity. I made half a dozen suggestions. But he must've seen my shake."

"Your shake?" Soraya asked.

"I've been doing a little blow, on the off-hours, of course. But I had to get high and clear for the meeting."

"Shit," Soraya said. Her voice was suddenly lofty, and she felt her mother's disappointment come through, her disdain for anyone who acted out of weakness.

"That's not the point; that I fucked up is not the point," Gus said. "He was all like, Forget ever doing any legitimate work for me. But there is one job you could do. It was ugly work, and I'm not in that much trouble. So of course I said no."

"What job?"

"I can't tell you that," Gus said.

Soraya stared at him. With one finger she slid first her own drink and then his out of their reach on the windowsill. "Gus, this is important. What job?"

"I wish I could tell you, but right now, I don't feel like I can trust you."

"Gus . . ." She felt confusion surround her. The party noise had peaked—the other room was wild with music and people yelling. Soon enough one or both of the Apple cousins would show up. And that was the whole point, wasn't it? But it was taking an awfully long time.

She stared at Gus and felt that she loved him. But she was working. Either way, she had to know. "Gus, honey, I love you. I'm going to stand by you and get you through this thing no matter what. Just because you weren't like this when we met doesn't mean I can't love you through it. But you have to tell me what Simon Apple said to you. This isn't about us, it's about people dying."

"And you and the Novak boys have a client," Gus said. "And you need to solve that double murder so you can get paid."

"How'd you know that?" Soraya asked.

"This room at the Sutherland? Whatever, Soraya, I'm not

stupid." Gus stood up. "I'm not saying you're working for one of the Apples, but you might as well be. And they are not clean. I can tell you that for sure."

Gus grabbed his coat from the bed and wrestled with it. He took his tequila from the windowsill, finished it, and the ice banged his lips. Then he grabbed Soraya's drink and finished that, too.

He said, "I've got to get out of here."

"Gus, wait," Soraya said. She was looking at his beautiful face, his eyes all watery and desperate now, his lower lip bitten and ragged. She even saw that his shoes were messy, that the cuffs of his pants were frayed from where they'd dragged on the street. She reached out, but he was already stepping back from her, three feet, then five.

"I'll call you when I'm good," he said.

"When will that be?" Soraya asked. "Please, Gus. I don't want to lose you."

"Maybe I will take that job," Gus said, and he sounded resigned. "I really don't know how else I'm going to make it."

And then, before Soraya could say anything else, he was out of the bedroom and gone.

Soraya waited a moment before wandering back into the party. The couches had been pushed into a corner and there was dancing. Soraya joined in, put her hands up in the air. Save crying, she couldn't think what else to do. She got another drink, too, and only reassured herself that in the morning, so much more would be clear.

"Seems I've survived till the end," Edwige said when everyone else had gone, at about three in the morning. By then Felix was back on the couch, sipping whiskey and staring out at the charcoal-colored sky above Central Park.

"Stay here if you like," Soraya said.

Edwige looked from her to Felix and back again.

"No, I'll leave you two lovebirds alone," she said. "Besides, I think Morris Apple is waiting for me in the private bar they keep downstairs behind the Lido."

"I didn't know about that," Soraya said.

"Maybe he said private car, not bar. I forget."

"Don't you want to be careful with him?" Soraya asked. "He seems all riled up about something."

"Morris?" Edwige asked. She laughed. "He's the biggest pussycat in the world. He wouldn't hurt a girl like me. In fact, I doubt he'll even kiss me good night. All he'll do is tell me his problems and put his head in my lap. Now go to sleep, you two, and hold each other tight as you can."

And she went out.

Felix stood up. He dragged the couches back into place but did nothing with the rest of the room. Soraya thought he might be a somber drunk, cold and calculating. She couldn't imagine how to begin to say that she wanted him to hold her, because she felt on the brink of tears.

"I saw Gus on his way out," Felix said. He went to the closet then and pulled out a soft blue blanket. He threw it over the couch and stepped out of his boots. His movements weren't steady. He wasn't looking at Soraya.

"So," Soraya said.

"He didn't look good."

"I know."

"It's hard for anybody to beat their history. But guys like him, sometimes I wonder if it's possible at all."

"Thanks," Soraya said. "Thanks a lot for that."

She turned then and went quickly into the bedroom, slamming the doors behind her.

"Soraya," Felix called after her. "Wait. That was stupid. I'm sorry."

"Don't be," Soraya called out. "I know perfectly well that my choices and their outcomes are all my fault."

"Wow," he said. "Somebody sure didn't have a good time at their own party."

Felix stared at the closed doors to the bedroom. The thin strip of light at the bottom of the door suddenly went out.

11 On Monday, Franklin's phone rang at six in the morning. He climbed over Jenny Hurly to get it and then stood at his window, looking down at the city. He'd never spent so much time at home before.

"Franklin?" Starling Furst called out.

"Yeah," Franklin said.

"Two deaths last night, both in Apple properties."

"Not the Sutherland," Franklin said. He looked down at Jenny's sleeping form, the height of her hip under the sheets. His prayer was silent as he waited for the answer.

"Copycat thing in the Sperling, down on East Thirty-second Street. Then a woman fell down an elevator shaft in a York Avenue condo the Apples just converted."

"Could've been an accident, the second one," Franklin said.

"The police aren't going to treat it that way," Starling said. "You talk to your clients?"

Franklin shook his head. Since when did his ex–father-in-law have an investment in his business?

"Look, thanks for the call," Franklin said. "We'll get on it."

"Let me know if there's anything I can do," Starling said, and hung up.

It was interesting, Franklin thought, to have such a powerful ally. But he knew the calls would stop coming the moment Ellie disappointed Starling again and didn't come to New York. It didn't matter, Franklin thought. Somewhere inside him, Starling Furst must have known that you could never put love back together once you'd broken it apart.

"What's up?" Jenny asked. She sat up in bed. She was naked, and she stretched, yawned wide. Her hair was messy and stood up in all directions.

"Two more murders."

"Felix and Soraya okay?"

"Yeah."

"Then come here," she said. And Franklin did. But he checked the clock first. He knew he didn't have much time.

Franklin sat down with Gennardi and Philip at the Eden coffee shop on East Sixty-eighth and Madison. It was Monday morning, around 10 A.M.

"What?" Gennardi said.

"How's your cheap room at the Sperling?" Franklin asked.

"Cheap," Gennardi said. "Why?"

"Where are you sleeping these days?" Franklin asked Philip.

"I keep two rooms," Philip said simply. Franklin knew not to ask Philip more about his freelance work for African governments. He didn't need to know more, and he would've had a hard time following who was good and who wasn't in the Horn of Africa in any case. So when Philip said he kept two rooms, he meant that he kept two lives. And it was just safer for everyone if they didn't know where he lived when he wasn't with them.

"Last night wasn't good for people who stay in Apple properties. Two deaths. The Sperling and a new condo on York Avenue. The Sperling was a smash-and-grab in a penthouse. A guy was the victim. The condo has twenty floors, twenty multimillion-dollar apartments. This lady who just bought two fell down the elevator shaft. The thing in the Sperling was more straightforward."

"That uptown loft project?" Gennardi asked.

"I guess so," Franklin said. "What do you know about the Sperling?"

"Lot of backpackers, mostly European. The place could use a renovation. What about the kids?" Gennardi said.

"They're okay," Franklin said. "I talked to them."

"What time was the murder?"

"Around 4 A.M.," Franklin said. "We can talk to Eitel Vasquez this afternoon. What's the matter with your faces?"

Gennardi was frowning. Philip wasn't. He only looked pensive.

"We were watching the Sutherland and we saw Gus come out of there," Gennardi said.

"Gus Moravia?" Franklin asked. "Soraya's boyfriend? So?"

"He got into a car with Simon Apple," Philip said. "And they went south, but we didn't follow them. The cops didn't, either. They wouldn't know Gus, and they're not going to follow Simon."

"Why not?"

"Come on, Franklin. Simon's rich," Gennardi said.

"What time was this?" Franklin asked.

"Three-thirty."

The three men were quiet. The waitress came over and delivered eggs, poured coffee.

"It could mean nothing," Franklin said.

"That Gus," Philip said. "He always gets caught up with the wrong people."

"The kind of wrong people who usually do the wrong kind of things," Gennardi said.

"Let's not jump quite yet," Franklin said. "Gus is always popping up where he's not wanted. He's like a gopher. We have clients, and we need to solve their problem. Not every single other thing."

Gennardi and Philip were quiet. Franklin watched them. He knew they were all thinking the same thing. Four deaths and one murderer. No suspects. Forget the client. They needed to move much, much faster. Before anyone else was killed.

"Every single other thing is going to turn into our client's problem, and fast," Philip said. "Barring some surprise, that's always the way."

Franklin and Gennardi looked at each other. They hadn't understood Philip, who often liked to speak in parables.

"I mean that we can't ignore the fact that we saw Simon and Gus last night," Philip said.

"I don't need any more heartbreak for Soraya Navarro. Here's what we're doing. You two watch the Apples. I'm going down to the Sperling to talk to Vasquez. I'll have Felix with me," Franklin said. "Let's hustle."

"We agree it's a thing with the Apples," Eitel Vasquez said to Franklin. They stood in the street outside the Sperling with Felix. There was still police tape around the hotel lobby. The killer had run out the front door and caught a cab, simple as that.

"Let's say . . . we don't need to disagree on that," Franklin said.

"Jesus, Franklin, we're not fucking lawyers," Vasquez said. Franklin laughed suddenly. He watched his son, who looked like he hadn't slept in days.

"Sorry," Franklin said. "Okay—lemme tell you what I've got."

Franklin ran through some of his information—about the Apples, their history, and what was going on between the cousins. He left out what Gennardi and Philip had told him about Gus and Simon. He wasn't sure what to make of that, not yet, anyway.

Felix stood with them and listened, but after he'd met Eitel, he hadn't said much. He felt very careful with cops after Mike Sharpman had acted like a friend and then turned out to be the exact opposite. And frankly, Vasquez didn't look too interested in him, either. Felix stared at the Sperling. They could see the lobby through the windows— there was a large group of ugly green lounge chairs that looked like blobs, and next to each one of them was a black steel side table. Felix thought it looked like three-dimensional diagrams of plant cells. Biology turned into furniture.

"Take it one more step with me," Vasquez said. "It's an employee, say. And he's angry and he's taking a thing out on the Apples and making a little money, too."

"What'd the killer get off the vic this time?" Franklin asked.

"Gold chain, wallet. Four thousand dollars, cash. That's what we told the press. The truth is that the killer took the guy's room card, went in, and got a couple of hundred grand worth of jewelry. Then he left. The way I see it, somebody on staff engineered this, same as the Sutherland deal. The payoff was what was in the room. Somebody knew there was a haul there and they phoned it in."

"The woman in the elevator?" Franklin asked.

"Forty blocks away and eighty minutes earlier. We've got a killer on a high, and we've got somebody moving him around. Two killings, two fat payoffs. He grabbed a shitload of jewels off the old lady, too. Now our boy'll go quiet for a week or so, just like last time. Only difference is that the fucker lied. When he said he'd strike *this place* again, he meant *these places*—he meant Apple properties. See? We got a young guy who's desperate and he's taking directions from somebody. Now we're waiting for a phone call from someone who wants to say who did what."

"You're moving too fast for me," Franklin said. "Take it easy. I'm older than you."

Vasquez watched him. He didn't say anything and folded his arms over his leather trench.

"I'm forty-five. You're what? Forty-seven? Don't tell me how quick to move. I don't like you, Franklin," Vasquez said. "And I don't give a shit about your boy here or your legacy. But when the Apples do their reveal, which should be any day now, they'll do it to you. They fucked somebody hard, and that's why this is happening. I'm close, but I don't know exactly who it is. You'll find out. You'll tell me."

"You're pushing," Felix said suddenly. He'd gotten between his father and Vasquez, as if he were going to defend his father against the detective.

Vasquez smiled. "Your boy is impulsive," he said. "He's hotheaded, like a little newbie cop. He needs to lose that feature, quick."

Vasquez turned away then, ducked under the yellow tape, and went into the Sperling. The uniforms who'd watched all this glared at Felix and Franklin.

"Fuck him, huh?" Felix said. He had to move quickly to follow his father down the street.

Franklin ignored Felix. He turned suddenly and smiled at his son. He said, "I got us round-trip tickets to see our clients. Tomorrow, 6 A.M. I'll leave the particulars on your voice mail. I'll see you in the morning."

Franklin gripped his son's arm as if he were about to say something else, but then he seemed to think better of it. He turned and walked away.

Felix stood there, on the corner of East Thirty-second and Park Avenue South. He watched his father disappear around a corner. He reached for his phone. But he realized he had no one to call. Soraya was angry with him. He wasn't sure what he ought to say to Lanie. Did he miss her? Need her? He didn't know.

He started to walk north toward the Sutherland.

*   *   *

Soraya sat in a brocade easy chair in the bedroom at the Sutherland. She'd been trying to figure out for the last half hour how to tell Franklin what Gus had said without creating a situation where Franklin felt like he needed to get to Gus. Every part of her wanted to keep from betraying Gus's trust. But two more people were dead and something was very, very wrong.

Though the maids had cleaned extensively, the room still smelled of cigarettes and alcohol from the party the night before. She got up suddenly and threw on her black shearling coat. She felt the outline of the snub-nosed Glock 33, the "Lady Glock" she kept inside the tear-away lining and that made her feel a bit better. She'd grabbed it from her dorm room the day before, along with the coat and some underwear. As she waited for the elevator, her phone beeped. Felix. She didn't answer it. She was too tense to talk to him, too bothered by how far apart they were. What she needed, she realized, was a father to talk to. What she had was Franklin.

She walked through the lobby and out to the street. She figured she'd find a diner, get a chicken sandwich and some tea, try to work through her concerns.

"Soraya?"

She looked up. Morris Apple. The stupid cousin, she thought. The sucker who liked to tell Edwige all his problems. He was wearing a black corduroy suit that was buttoned tight around his middle and a too bright white-and-orange-checked shirt.

"Hungry?" he asked. She smiled.

"You read my mind," she said.

"There's a place down the street called Swifty's where they make a great roast beef club," Morris said.

"I was thinking chicken," Soraya said.

"Oh—that's what I meant," Morris said. He grinned, and he had dimples like a five-year-old.

Before they turned around, Soraya saw Philip and Gennardi double-parked across the street. She winked at them, long. Cover me.

Philip and Gennardi hadn't moved since breakfast. They'd watched the exchange, and now they crept along after Soraya and Morris as they walked down Madison.

"It wouldn't occur to her that he's been waiting outside for her all day," Philip said.

"She's a pro," Gennardi said. "That fat fucker's bubbling with information. And she's going to take it."

"She's good," Philip said.

"She's got the work in her blood," Gennardi said. He dialed Franklin's number to tell him what had happened. This was always how it worked—so long as Franklin was given every available piece of the puzzle, eventually he'd fit them together.

"Time to let the bald mastermind know the score," Philip said.

Gennardi nodded. "I don't get any of it yet, but I'd say we'll have a solution by Wednesday, the latest."

"I sure wish we had somebody following Simon Apple," Philip said.

"All that handsome boy does is work and dip with the ladies," Gennardi said. "This Morris, though—he runs around like an electrocuted chicken." Then Gennardi started laughing and burping. He said, "You get that one?"

Swifty's was nearly empty and they were led to a white leather banquette in the back. It was just before noon, and the Monday lunchtime crowd hadn't yet begun to stream in. Soraya sniffled. She wondered if she might be getting a cold.

She wanted to talk to Gus. And she didn't know where the hell he was.

"Let me help you with your coat," Morris said. Soraya slipped it off and handed it to him, and Morris laid it next to his blazer and then scooted over to the middle of the banquette.

"You heard about what happened last night," Morris said. Soraya nodded. A waitress appeared and filled their water glasses and set out bread and olive oil. They didn't begin to speak until she left.

Soraya said, "Why would someone do such a thing?" And she hoped that sounded remotely genuine. Morris stared at her. His clothes were very fine, but he seemed oblivious. Crumbs from the bread he was eating covered his shirt and pants.

"When I was younger, I used to fly me and a bunch of my friends down to Indianapolis for the 500, and we'd go to the trashy races they had around the big race—you remind me of the flag girls, you know? The ones who whip the flag around and then the cars take off?"

"They still have those?" Soraya asked. Morris nodded. She wondered if he was intentionally trying to offend her— or was he trying to appear more manly than he really was?

"Yeah. You look like one of those girls."

Their sandwiches arrived. Morris ate with intense concentration. He used dabs of condiments and he was quick with his napkin. He cleaned his plate before she'd even gotten started and she wondered if he'd order another. His lips were wet and gleaming and he stared around the empty restaurant.

Soraya said, "This is really good. I wonder if they make an extra effort because it's you."

But Morris seemed not to hear her. She had one question that she thought she could actually ask. She wanted to know what he'd meant when he said he and his cousin disagreed about how to deal with the police the other night when they'd been driving through the park. But she didn't want to scare him off.

"I may not seem that bright," Morris said, "but someday I'll be running this whole organization. You know that, don't you?"

Soraya nodded. She pretended as if her mouth were full, gestured that he should keep talking. He ran a finger over the flat of his plate, slipped what few bits of food he found into his mouth.

He said, "I know I seem young, but you do, too. And I think . . . I wonder if we might ever really go out. You know, what I want to impress upon you here is that I'm . . ."

He seemed confused, searching for a word. Soraya's nose twitched. She'd expected the come-on, but not the interest in business.

"Ambitious," she said.

"That's right," he said. "That's it. Do you think we could get together? Or are you really serious with the boyfriend you mentioned?"

"It's casual. No big thing."

"You Dominicans are terrific that way," he said.

And she said nothing to that, either. She was a hundred percent Puerto Rican, but no one ever asked about it. They just assumed something and said it.

Then Morris was ordering dessert. He didn't even look at her. He was focused on the food. He was waiting for it and his hands kept moving around, searching. He seemed incredibly lonely, even slightly deranged.

"You just watch me. Me and Simon are going to make Apple and Apple into something huge. You might want to come along for the ride—be my flag girl, you know. My Dominican flag girl."

Soraya took her napkin, waved it around in the air as if she were starting a race.

"Yes! Like that."

"I've got your number. Now could I get some tea?" she asked. "I need to go in just a few minutes, but I'd love to get warm first."

Morris looked around for the waiter. His hand wandered off the table and down to her thigh, as if it had no connection to his brain. She picked it up and put it back on the table, and he didn't even look her way. He kept fidgeting, moving about in the booth like the springs were jabbing into his butt.

She thought, Whatever Simon promised him for saying nothing, it wasn't enough. He was too stupid. She thought that soon, Simon would kill him.

12

Felix got his Roadrunner out of the lot and drove uptown to his father's place to pick him up and go to LaGuardia Airport. He hardly ever got a chance to use the car these days; he usually just left it parked in a lot over in Chelsea. The attendant at the lot owed Franklin a favor from way back, when Franklin had helped him beat a manslaughter charge, so Felix only had to pay fifty bucks a month. Sometimes he went over and napped in the car, and he waxed it, too. But he drove it less and less. Still, he didn't want to let it go. He loved that car. They drove in silence to the airport and the plane ride was just as quiet. It was terribly early on Tuesday morning, and both men had worked through the day before, talking to people in Apple hotels. Neither had come up with anything.

A battered black Jeep was waiting for Franklin and Felix at the airport in Nashua. The driver was about seventy, gray haired, in a red hunting jacket. He didn't say anything during the forty-minute backwoods drive. The day was a brackish gray and it looked like it'd rain at any moment. The leaves had mostly fallen from the trees and it was far colder than it had been in the city. Both Franklin and Felix were in black trench coats and they wrapped them tightly around their bodies.

"You should wear a hat in the country," Felix said as he stared at his father's bald head. Felix settled his cowboy hat on his head. Franklin ignored him.

"Good day for shooting?" Franklin asked.

"They're all good days," the driver said, and lapsed back into silence.

"Doesn't like city folk," Franklin said to Felix. The man's back stiffened, but he still said nothing.

Felix watched the landscape.

"There's a wood doe," Felix said.

"What is?" Franklin asked.

"Bird that flew along there for a moment. I guess I know about fifty kinds of birds."

"What about that tree?" Franklin asked.

"Sycamore."

They fell silent again and looked at the bare, unforgiving landscape.

"Damn shame they wouldn't let me bring my new Magnum on the plane."

"You like that model?" the old driver asked, suddenly interested. "I'm saving up for one now. Like carrying a cannon in your hand is what they say. Take down anything the forest has to offer."

"But I use it to blow down a door," Franklin said, "never to knock over a bear."

"Packs plenty of punch whatever you use it for, that's for sure," the driver said as they pulled through a gate.

He waved to a man in a guardhouse, who came and checked Franklin and Felix's ID. He had a handgun strapped to his waist. Felix looked around. On either side of the gate was a dozen feet of steel fencing, topped with razor wire. He thought it looked like they were entering a prison, not a hunting resort. They drove for another half mile and parked in front of a massive camp house.

"Mr. Wallingford and Mr. Stowe said they'd like you to come down to Huckleberry Pond. Follow me," the driver said. They walked behind the old man down a beaten path. After several minutes they arrived at a bluff that overlooked a quiet pond. The hollow, messy sound of a shotgun release muddied the quiet every few moments. They walked past a few older men who were loading their guns, talking quietly about their kills.

Ed Wallingford and Tom Stowe were in a private blind with an assistant who was tending to their equipment. They were in great green waders and dark brown coats, their wool hats pulled low over their ears. They looked over once as Franklin and Felix approached.

"Hello there," Ed Wallingford said. He pulled off his hat, and his white hair stood out in the landscape like a puff of smoke or a low-slung cloud. He stepped out of the bog.

"Let's let Tom shoot before we talk. He hasn't had much luck today," Ed Wallingford said.

They turned then and watched Tom take aim at some grass about thirty yards away. He shot, the noise echoed, and Franklin and Felix covered their ears. But then a duck paddled for a moment and took off into the air twenty feet to the right. Its frenzied call sounded hopeful, even defiant.

"Mind if I try?" Franklin asked. Ed didn't smile. He merely handed over his gun.

"It's sighted for me, but have fun with it," he said. "You're smaller, so aim six or seven degrees down from where you normally would."

Franklin took the gun and squatted down. While he did so, Tom Stowe clambered up from the mud and steadied himself. He observed everything, handed his gun to the teenage assistant. As usual, he didn't say a word.

Franklin sighted. He aimed at a rustle in some brush far across the pond. Felix watched and didn't speak. He'd hunted some on his mother's property, shot wolves and other scavengers, but he'd never done it for sport. His father sent a round into the brush, and there was a squawk. A few seconds later a duck paddled away, quacking indignantly.

He stood slowly and handed back the gun.

"Nice shooting," Ed said.

"Thanks," Franklin said. "I suppose I'd have to take a few

more potshots like that before I was tuned up to go for the kill."

"That's always the way," Ed said. "Now, what've you got for us?"

"Well," Franklin said. "You were right. What occurred has nothing to do with you or your families."

Felix shivered suddenly in the wind. None of the men looked at him. Tom Stowe sucked air through his teeth.

"Explain it," Ed said.

"Two more deaths the night before last. One murder-robbery that went the same way as your tragedy and an accident, both on Apple properties. It's something with the Apples. We're just not sure what yet."

"But you saw them," Ed said.

"You have somebody watching me?" Franklin asked.

"We're working with a lot of people."

Franklin frowned. "You don't have to trust me. But if you second-guess me, I don't need to work for you."

The four men stared at each other. Franklin sighed. He looked over the pond. He said, "I take you on as a client, I work for you exclusively. I have my people, my son here and some others. We do what we can. But how we go about it is up to us."

"It's all right," Ed said. "Police commissioner mentioned you moved your people into the Sutherland, that's all. You couldn't do that without seeing the Apples."

"I only take one client at a time, as I said."

"That's fine," Ed said.

"Somebody's trying to ruin the Apples. And they want to do it fast. And they're stupid about it. Stupid and merciless. They'll go too far and show themselves, and I'll be there or my people will."

"We just want a name and a little proof," Ed said.

Franklin looked at Tom Stowe. The man hadn't stopped staring at him.

"Thanks for the gun," Franklin said. "I do like my handguns."

"What does your boy use?"

"An automatic," Felix said. "Smith & Wesson .45."

"Army issue. We like that."

"We should have something for you in two or three days."

"Don't make it longer than that," Tom said. "I want to go home soon. And grieve about my wife in peace. But first I want some justice."

"You'll have it."

While Felix went to get the Roadrunner from the eight-hour parking lot at LaGuardia, Franklin bought some newspapers. It was late afternoon. Franklin and Felix had had lunch with the Texans in the dining room at the main house. They'd eaten venison and discussed guns, justice, and police commissioners.

Felix came up in the Roadrunner and several people glanced at the car. The carburetor need adjusting, so the big engine rumbled like a diesel truck.

"Jesus, look at this," Franklin said once he'd gotten in and settled himself. He had the *Spectator* in his fists and he was looking at an article on page eight. Morris Apple had spoken out about the multiple killings at Apple properties. It was an interview, and it read as if he'd initiated it. He said that he'd been urging Stuart Apple to make the properties safer for some time, that this was a new era for hotels and private residences and that reforms needed to be created lest additional murders occur. The interview read as if somebody had met with Morris, constructed his responses, and Morris had delivered his lines from a cue card. Morris was urging that people not stay in Apple properties for the foreseeable future until the safety issue had been sorted out. Eitel Vasquez was quoted, too. He said that the police had the issue under control, that it wasn't an issue of private safety. In a sidebar there was a note saying a lengthier piece on Eitel Vasquez would be published on Sunday.

"Who wrote it?" Felix asked.

"Lanie. You need to go see her. Do it tonight or tomorrow, the latest. Jesus," Franklin repeated.

He called Gennardi.

"You still sleeping in town?" Franklin asked.

"Eating a Sperling club sandwich right now," Gennardi said. "What's up?"

Franklin thought for a moment. He could hear the TV going in the background in Gennardi's hotel room.

"We need to watch this Morris kid," Franklin said. He covered the receiver, turned to Felix. He said, "Call Soraya." Felix did.

"Yeah, I read the paper," Gennardi said. "Philip is out looking for him now. The kid lives in his dead father's town house. His mother died from pills when he was about nineteen. He stays in their bedroom."

"Maudlin," Franklin said.

"Yeah, a real fucking loser."

"But is he stupid?" Franklin asked. "Because then somebody else is designing this mess or he's just taking advantage of Eitel Vasquez's disgruntled employee theory."

"I have no idea if he's stupid. But if he thinks his uncle killed his father and he's been stewing about that since he was a preteen, then he's a suspect."

"Nah," Franklin said. "Doesn't jibe right. He'd just kill the old guy. Didn't you say Soraya hung out with him yesterday?"

"They had lunch. He said things to her."

"Felix will talk to her. Then we'll meet with Eitel Vasquez tomorrow."

"I'll call you," Gennardi said.

Franklin and Felix passed into Manhattan.

Felix got off the phone with Soraya. He said, "She's okay. I'm going to call Lanie now."

Franklin rubbed his stubbled cheeks, thought about stopping at Zitto's and giving Karen a warning. But he knew how much value that kind of thing had. He called Jenny Hurly. She was already at his house, half asleep, waiting for him to come home.

After Felix dropped his father off uptown, he drove down to the West Village. He parked in a twenty-dollar-an-hour lot, cursed the expense, and stepped into Pippa's, where he was supposed to meet Lanie.

He took a table near the door. Pippa's had only been open for a few months, and it was right near Lanie's apartment. It was tiny, with fewer than a dozen tables and a small bay window in the front with a curtain over it. There was a fire in the back and a nice older lady, who served only a few sorts of drinks—a rum punch, a gin fizz, a couple of other things with names that amused her and reminded her of her youth. Lanie had written about it before she'd gotten put on the city hall beat.

Lanie came in. She was all in black and looked professional, with a pair of small gold hoop earrings. Her great mess of curly brown hair was pulled back. She clutched her bag so tightly that it looked like she was afraid someone was going to steal it from her.

"I've missed you," Lanie said.

"Now you're friendly," Felix said.

"Oh, Felix," Lanie said. She hadn't touched him, and when Pippa came up, Lanie jumped up and hugged her, ordered two martinis the Pippa way, which meant straight gin in a water glass with a tablespoon of crushed ice.

"What's the matter?" Lanie asked when she sat down again. Felix couldn't think of the right thing to say, so he was quiet. Finally he said, "What about the Apple property killings? What's going on with that?"

"I was about to ask you the same question," Lanie said.

"You know I can't talk to you about business."

"Even just a hint? I can tell you what I've learned about Morris and Simon."

"What about them?" Felix said.

"Morris is stupid and Simon wants to run the whole show and he will someday, if he and his father force Morris out. That's the deal. Simon's a bit of a playboy."

"He tries to date models, that sort of thing," Felix said. "Why don't you tell me something I don't know?" He looked at her neck, her clavicle. He remembered kissing her.

"He tries to. He's not Donald Trump, but I think that if his father let him, he'd try to be. He's only twenty-four. Both boys are. They're allowed to control an awful lot of wealth for twenty-four. Now tell me, who would want to destroy them? The unions? The same people who caused all the trouble for that nice Cipriani family?"

"I can't talk about it," Felix said. "I said that."

"You're not being fun."

"Four people have been killed. We're looking for a murderer."

"I know that, Felix." She said his name like she was taunting him, like this was fifth grade. Then they were both quiet. She said, "I'm also talking to Eitel Vasquez. Your grandfather put me on to him. It's occurred to me that taking down the Apples wouldn't be the worst thing for Starling Furst. Families who own real estate never mind when other real estate families fall apart."

"Don't be stupid," Felix said.

"See," Lanie said, and her voice was singsong, "even though we're not together right now, I'm all up in your shit."

"I see that," Felix said. "And I can't say it's the best feeling. Where I'm from, you're either with someone or you're not. It's not about 'right now.'"

Lanie frowned. She said, "You're from New York originally. That's how you are inside. Anyway, let's not get into that. Let's talk about fun stuff instead."

"Like murder," Felix said. He shook his head. "You want to make it hard for me to like you, you're succeeding."

Lanie's face was flat. He saw her check her watch, her cute little nose twitching slightly. He remembered how sweet she'd been when he first woke up at her house so many months ago and had no idea where he was. The idea of her waking up with someone else there hurt him.

"It's looking more and more like we've got a real New York City relationship," Lanie said.

"You mean we spend our time together figuring out what we can get from each other?"

"That. And when you get angry with me, both of us know it's just because you can't be with the person you really love."

Felix looked away. He only felt cold. Lanie's phone rang then, and she held on to it.

"Of course your phone would ring right now," Felix said.

"Don't be dramatic, Felix," she said. "It doesn't suit you, and my phone rings all the time. That's how I like it. I'm going to go now. I'll be in touch when I know something."

She got up from the bar then and took the call.

Late on Tuesday night Soraya went to meet Gus down at Suite 16. He'd found some unsteady work as a doorman because one of his buddies was throwing parties at the club.

He had a half hour break at 1 A.M. and they'd agreed to see each other then. She came up to the club and found him there, deep in conversation with a tall actor whom she recognized from some Spike Lee movies. He seemed to be the other doorman.

She waited for them to finish talking. Gus wore a black leather trench coat and a black turtleneck, which looked unfamiliar to Soraya, but she knew it was standard doorman clothing. His skin seemed awfully pale, and she hoped it was just set off by all the black.

"Hi, baby," Gus said. He saw four girls behind Soraya and opened the velvet rope for them. They thanked him by name. Soraya thought they looked about fifteen.

Soraya said, "Where are we going to go?"

Gus turned and nodded to the actor, who took over his post in front of the black-lacquered door to the club. More people were coming up, in groups of two and three. But it was a quiet night.

"This way," Gus said. He headed west on West Sixteenth Street toward the meat market district.

"You want to go to Casanis?" Soraya asked.

"I don't know if we have time. I have to meet a guy."

Soraya felt the wind whipping down toward them from the river, and she wanted very much not to be able to understand what Gus was talking about.

"A guy?" Soraya asked. Gus kept licking his lips, and suddenly Soraya noticed that his tongue was able to reach awfully far out. Freakishly far.

"I need to, Soraya. If you don't want to do this with me, we can talk later, tomorrow or something."

She stopped. They were in the middle of a quiet block. A factory took up most of the south side of the street. And there were brownstones and cheap apartment buildings on the north side. There were no leaves on the trees. There wasn't a person coming in either direction. No cars moved. They'd been walking awfully fast.

"Look, Gus, what did Simon ask you to do the other night?"

"I don't want to tell you that," Gus said. "It's not important. I said I wouldn't do it, so it's not an issue."

"It is important. Something's wrong with those Apples and two more people died. This isn't a joke, Gus."

"I didn't say it was," Gus said. He stopped suddenly and tugged up the sleeve of his coat, tried to read an address he'd written on his forearm by the dim beam coming down from a streetlight. She watched him curse.

"Nobody said anything was a joke," Gus muttered. "For your own safety, I can't tell you. The guy I'm supposed to meet, he'll come in a car. He's going to stop in front of a house up this way. A little farther."

"My safety?" Soraya asked. She laughed. "You've got me out on the street at one in the morning and we're waiting for somebody to come and sell you drugs because you've blown out your club connections and you're worried about my safety?"

"Hey, quiet down now," Gus said. He looked quickly up and down the street as if he were afraid she'd alienate his connection. Soraya laughed again, but it came out as more of a choking noise.

"Fuck this," she said. "You're a joke, you know that? You're the only guy I ever loved and you're trading it all in for drugs, when you swore to me you'd never go that way!"

"Soraya—," Gus said. He was backing away from her.

"If you love me, then come with me," Soraya said. She moved east, back the way they'd come, stepping backward, feeling her way. Gus didn't move.

"Come with me," Soraya said again. But Gus just shook

his head. She could even tell that he was looking somewhere beyond her, over her shoulder.

And Soraya had to be tough, so she turned away, and though she was crying, she laughed again. She walked as slow as she could, praying that he'd follow. Instead she watched a shiny black dial-a-car drift by her. The driver looked her over, as if he was looking for someone who would be waiting in front of a specific house. She knew the driver was the only person who mattered to Gus now. She didn't look back.

Soraya caught an F train and took it up to West Fifty-ninth Street; then she walked east along Central Park South. It was past four on Wednesday morning and the streets were quiet. She told herself that she felt good and free, and she knew it was a lie. When she got to the Sutherland, Felix was still up, watching TV in the bedroom. He'd been lying on the bed.

She said, "Don't get up. We can both stay in here."

"I'm good with the couch," Felix said. He stood up. He was still watching the television. She looked. There were a lot of large men in big chairs, and they were laughing. It was a show about the NFL.

"Please," she said. "Just turn that off and sleep with me here."

She slipped off her jeans and her shirt and saw Felix work hard not to look at her. But she was too tired to care. She closed her eyes, listened to Felix take off his pants. She felt him lie down on the bed, far away from her.

"What's the matter?" Felix asked.

"I'm not sure," she said.

They were quiet. There was no sound in the room. The sheets smelled of wildflowers.

Soraya said, "Tomorrow we should meet with Franklin.

Morris Apple told me something that I need to share."

"Okay," Felix said. "Tomorrow."

Felix had a nightmare. He'd gone to sleep out in an alley with a beautiful woman. A dangerous man had lingered nearby. In the morning the beautiful woman took him to a store for bread. But in the store the woman disappeared. He looked out the window and the dangerous man was hustling her away.

He was screaming, "I had it in my hand," when Soraya woke him up. She held his head in her arms for a few minutes, quieted him down.

In the morning they pretended as if this had not happened.

13

Franklin and Gennardi met Eitel Vasquez at a diner in Jackson Heights at six-thirty on Wednesday morning. It was the only time Vasquez would give them. His daughter worked at the place as a waitress, and he liked to drive her in and then have her serve him coffee.

"I doubt it," Eitel Vasquez said when Franklin told him about Morris Apple and about what Soraya had said about him not understanding why his brother, Simon, wasn't cooperating with the police. "Not impossible, but I doubt he's doing anything really wrong. We got a family of Dominicans on 118th Street with a *papi* who went missing two days ago. He worked in the laundry room at the Gershwin, and he used to work at the Sutherland. He's tall and thin."

"You going to bring him in?" Franklin asked.

Vasquez looked at Franklin like he was a beat cop who'd just taken a french fry out of a murder victim's grip and eaten it.

"Yes, we're going to bring him in," Vasquez said. "But he doesn't know we're on to him yet. We watched him all last night."

"What'd he do?" Franklin asked.

"First he had some dinner. Then he killed a guy," Vasquez said, and laughed. Vasquez's daughter, Emilia, came to the table. She delivered eggs and corned beef hash for Vasquez, cream of wheat for Gennardi, and burnt rye toast for Franklin, which was the way he'd asked for it. She was a knockout, with inch-long eyelashes and a deep cleavage that pressed up against the V in her T-shirt when she bent over to refill their coffees. Franklin and Gennardi made every effort not to look at her, because Vasquez was watching.

"How'd you get to the Dominican?" Franklin asked.

"Like I'm telling you that," Vasquez said. "Gimme a second here to stop my laughing, because I want to make sure I get all the details straight before I tell you every single one of them."

"Family gave him up?"

"Fine," Vasquez said. "He missed work at the Gershwin. He's got priors. We did the rest."

"Seems dumb," Gennardi said.

"Criminals are," Vasquez said. He used his knife as a wall and piled food high on his fork and then crammed the fork against the knife before bringing the whole mess to his mouth.

"What about the headset, the directions?" Franklin asked.

"I'll ask him when we take him in—" Vasquez checked his watch. "In five minutes. But my bet is he's a religious man. He was getting his instructions on how to cure injustice from God. Tell your clients that's the end of it."

Franklin was on the outside of the booth, and he stood up. Gennardi slowly labored after him. When they were both standing, Franklin threw a five-dollar bill on the table.

"Thanks for your help," Franklin said.

"You think I'm wrong," Vasquez said.

"I think you're telling us about a third of what you know."

"Maybe," Vasquez said. He looked at his pager, which sat on the table next to the sugar. "We do have a guy in custody, though, as of now."

"Congratulations," Franklin said. "We're eager to meet him."

"When you got something for my case, then you can talk to my guy," Vasquez said, with his mouth full.

In the van Gennardi said, "Shit—would you drive me back down to the Sperling?"

"You forget something?" Franklin asked.

"Gun," Gennardi said. Franklin looked over at him. His black turtleneck was smudged with food, and his blazer was rumpled.

"Why don't you change, too? You don't want to start looking like me."

"Thanks."

They were on the West Side Highway, trucking along. For no reason, he thought about Jenny Hurly. And then he figured, what the hell. He probably ought to marry her. If she'd have him. It wasn't a beautiful moment to think such a thing, he realized, driving in a van with an unhappy partner who'd forgotten his gun and hadn't seen his kid and his wife in too many days, but that didn't keep it from being a beautiful thought, the kind of thought he'd had maybe two or three times before in his life, and none of those times had been in the last dozen years. So he closed his eyes for a second at the West Forty-second Street stoplight and cherished it.

There were several police cars in front of the Sperling. The morgue van was on the side street along with the crummy station wagon the chief of Manhattan forensics always drove in from Long Island. The entire area was cordoned off with yellow tape. Franklin double-parked next to a forlorn flower delivery van and sat still for a moment, looking at the busy crime scene.

"What would you call my expression?" Franklin asked.

"Baleful," Gennardi said.

"That's right. Because why?"

"They didn't do such a terrific job of picking the right unhappy ex-employee," Gennardi said.

"Maybe he did take somebody out and they did watch."

"Fucking cops," Gennardi said.

They got out of the van. Franklin looked up. The sky was the color of wet paper towels. When Franklin started around, he saw that Gennardi had recognized a sergeant he knew and he'd nodded at him.

Sergeant Mickens came over to them. He was a heavy black man, and he had an unhappy expression on his face, as if he'd looked away for a moment and someone had thrown his breakfast in the trash.

"They found a user in a Dumpster in the back with a bullet in his belly," Mickens said.

"The belly? One shot?" Gennardi asked.

Mickens nodded. "The user's single-round-is-all-you're-worth goodbye. They figure he moaned for a few hours and gave up the battle around dawn, when some guy from the laundry service got off work and flipped his personal garbage into the Dumpster. He said it didn't make the right sound. He looked in, saw a body, screamed, and managed to wake up some guests."

"Who was the vic? Not a guest of the hotel?"

"No, I don't have the name. Go down to the alley and check with Detective Vasquez. Maybe he'll talk to you."

"He's already here?"

"Busy little beaver must've taken the subway," Gennardi said. "Lord, I sure hope my gun is in my room."

They went down the alley and found Vasquez standing with Luke Ponset, a junior guy from forensics.

"This doesn't eliminate my suspect," Vasquez said when he saw them.

"I was hoping you wouldn't say that," Franklin said. "Who got it? A worker?"

"Nah, some guy . . . nightclub doorman or something." Vasquez looked down and checked his notepad.

"That's all you got?" Franklin said.

"Well, a bartender in the Blue Shade lounge in the Sperling ID'd the body right on the spot. I guess she stays open till dawn some nights, though we're not going to let her do that anymore. Said it was a guy who used to work for Terrence Cheng. He ran Eden-Roc."

"Gus Moravia?" Franklin asked.

"Yeah, that's the name. How'd you guess?" Vasquez seemed genuinely impressed. Then he said, "What's your angle, Novak?"

"You come clean with me, I'll give you what I know. Nothing till then," Franklin said. He watched Vasquez's mouth twitch.

The team from forensics was carefully lifting the body out of the Dumpster. Franklin looked at it. There was Gus Moravia, dead.

Franklin said, "You know the ex-employee you've been watching is a bullshit lead."

"Maybe, maybe not," Vasquez said.

Gennardi had already gone around the corner to call Felix.

Felix and Soraya were up early on Wednesday because they were scheduled to meet Franklin at 10 A.M.

They'd woken up in the same bed. But neither mentioned that several times during the night, Soraya had held Felix and hushed him back to sleep. Instead Felix had hopped out of bed early, done push-ups and sit-ups in the living room, and then he'd taken a scalding shower, tried to slap the nightmare off his skin. While he shaved, he cast about desperately for the right phrase to show Soraya that his little nighttime freak-out didn't mean shit.

They ordered breakfast from room service.

"Why not?" Felix said. "It's free."

So they sat at the table and drank their coffee out of gilt-edged cups as they examined the morning papers and didn't speak, not about the case or about each other.

Soraya ate peeled grapefruit slices one at a time. They looked out at the bright sun over Central Park. Felix's cell rang. He looked and saw that it was Gennardi. He picked it up but waited a moment before answering.

Felix said, "Gennardi is lonely. He's having problems with Dianne."

"Why?" Soraya asked.

"He cheated on her. That's why he's staying at the Sperling. But nobody talks about it."

"I wish you hadn't told me that," Soraya said.

Felix took the call. He got up and went into the other room.

"Oh, God," Felix said. "That's not funny."

Soraya looked up. She'd never heard him sound quite like that before. Not since the first night when he'd been back, when he'd said he hadn't known what to do since he lost his sister. Soraya got up from the table. She pressed her fists against the hard surfaces of her ribs. She was dressed in brown pants and a midnight blue sweater with brown boots. Her hair was back in a ponytail. She took the ponytail out.

She said, "What?"

"Okay," Felix said; he was talking into the phone, but he was looking at her. "I'm not sure. I'll call in when I know."

Soraya tried a smile. Then that didn't work, so she stared. She said, "What is it?"

He got up close and she said it again, louder.

"Gus was killed last night."

She collapsed, but away from him. She didn't want to be held and then he was holding her up. She screamed.

He guided her a few steps away from the large glass-topped table. But then Soraya straightened up.

She said, "I'm going to the bathroom now."

"Leave the door open."

"Get the fuck away from me," she said. "I'm not going to kill myself. I'm going to throw up."

They walked back into the bedroom. And then she went into the master bathroom. Felix leaned against the door just outside the bathroom while Soraya bent over the toilet. She was sick for several minutes.

Through the door she said, "Let's go sit down for a minute on the couch. I want some orange juice. I don't suppose you'll let me out of your sight?"

Felix shook his head no.

Once they were seated, Felix called room service and asked for orange juice.

Soraya was looking at Felix and tears were running down her cheeks.

"When are we supposed to meet your father?" she asked.

"It doesn't matter."

"No. Let's meet in one hour. I want to move on this. I want to put away whoever did it. I want them gone."

"It's okay. I can stay here with you," Felix said.

"You waited when Penelope died," Soraya said. Then she didn't say anything else. Felix nodded. The orange juice came, and Felix took the two glasses from the steward's cart. While he signed, he watched Soraya. He sat down next to her on the couch, set the glasses on the coffee table. She drank for a moment, closed her eyes.

"Good," she said.

He put an arm around her back. She stood up suddenly and went to the window.

"I'm sorry," Felix said.

"I feel very cold. I laughed at him. When I saw him last night, I laughed at him and then I walked away."

"That doesn't matter."

She turned toward him quickly. Her eyelids were puffy.

She said, "Please don't try to touch me again. No matter what. Please."

"Okay."

He looked out at Central Park while she cried and he didn't move. She said, "I wish I had my shearling coat. It's the warmest thing I own and I can't find it. I must have left it in my dorm at school."

"Wear my coat."

"It's too big," she said. "Please don't try to help me right now."

An hour later Felix and Soraya sat in Franklin's office. Franklin watched the two of them. Philip and Gennardi were out trying to do something impossible. They were trying to watch Simon and Morris Apple at the same time, and they were also trying to hear whatever they could from Apple employees.

"They'll take turns sleeping in the van," Franklin said. "It's insane. Soraya, you should go home to your mother. If you don't call her, I will."

"You call her without my permission and you'll never see me again. Now let's talk about the case," Soraya said.

"You compartmentalize, just like your father," Franklin said.

"Big word for you," Soraya said.

"You could let us take care of this," Franklin said.

"So far you haven't done such a hot job," Soraya said. "Let's hear what you've got."

She sat hunched over, several feet away from Felix. She

was shivering. Franklin and Felix shifted uneasily as they watched her.

"Fair enough," Franklin said. "As far as the police are concerned, this death is unrelated. It looks to them like what it is."

"Which is?" Soraya asked.

Franklin frowned. He moved to slide open his desk drawer.

"Don't pull out a pistol and start playing with it," Soraya said. "Tell me what they think happened."

Franklin closed the drawer. He had a cup of cold coffee in front of him. Before he spoke, he took a sip of it.

"That this was a drug deal that went bad. Whoever Gus was dealing with threw him in a Dumpster. They believe the fact that the place was Apple owned and run was coincidence. I'm sorry, Soraya. I'm not going to tell the police they're wrong. Not yet. Now . . ." Franklin raised a finger, pointed at Soraya. "Be very honest here. Because it matters a lot. Was he using drugs or not?"

"He wasn't dealing," Soraya said. She didn't say anything else.

"For the police, these things are unrelated. They see no connection between Gus and the Apples. Zero. We know better. We need to start being extremely honest with each other."

"There's one thing I haven't mentioned," Soraya said.

"That Gus was a drug dealer?" Franklin asked. And Felix flashed his eyes at Franklin. *Go easy.*

"Sorry," Franklin said. He shook his head.

"I said he didn't deal. What the fuck—you think I'm lying to you? Three nights ago he came to the party we had at the Sutherland. He said Simon asked him to do something and he said no. He was freaked out about it."

"What was the thing?"

"He wouldn't tell me. It was for my own good that he wouldn't tell me. That's what he said."

Without looking, Soraya held her finger up in front of Felix.

"This is the truth?" Franklin asked.

"Of course it's the truth. You just asked me for the truth, didn't you? Gus is dead. You think I've got things I need to hold back?"

"You held that back."

"I didn't think it mattered," Soraya said. "Okay. That's a lie. I was protecting him. I was. I loved him."

Franklin got his new Magnum out from the drawer. He put it on his desk. He laid his hand on top of it.

"Now he's got the gun out," Soraya said. "Now he'll take the butt of it and scratch his tired old jaw."

"Gennardi and Philip saw Gus leave the Sutherland with Simon Apple three nights ago at the end of your party. That was ten, twenty minutes before those two murders occurred. See?"

"You think Gus is a murderer?" Soraya asked.

"I didn't say that," Franklin said. "I'm only talking about what I know. We're exchanging facts is what we're doing."

"Let's hear your side," Felix said. Soraya dug her hands into the seat. Then there was a moment when she didn't breathe.

Soraya said, "Simon is a smart little fucker. And he's evil. He wants to capitalize on these killings. Somebody did them, and it's screwing up his business, but he's smart and he knows that all he needs to do is wait and turn a bad thing into a good thing. So he's waiting. I think he wanted to pay Gus to kill Morris so Simon and his father would inherit everything. I think Gus said no."

"You're not saying that Simon's behind the killings that already happened," Franklin said.

"No. I don't know if he is or not."

"But what about the guy in the elevator taking directions, all that?"

"I don't care about that right now. All I know is one thing: If you ask somebody to kill someone and they say no, you don't have a lot of choices. What the fuck was Simon going to say to Gus? It's fine if you don't want to do it, just don't tell anybody? No—he had to kill him. So he did. And then he dumped the body behind an Apple property so whoever did the other killings would be the suspect."

"But the police don't agree," Franklin said.

"Just because the police don't see it my way doesn't mean I'm wrong. Gus left me last night and went to meet with a guy in a car. I thought Gus was buying drugs from the guy. Now I think the guy was supposed to kill him, or bring him to Simon, or both. It all comes back to what Simon asked him to do."

"And whether he did it," Franklin said.

"He didn't do anything," Soraya said.

Franklin rubbed his temples.

"Go home to your mother," he said.

"If I could, I'd laugh at you," Soraya said. Franklin watched her. Her lips were the wrong color, pale and pink, cracked. He thought they should have been red.

"There's one thing you could do," Franklin said.

Soraya looked at him.

"Morris Apple. He likes you. He took you for a ride and you two went to lunch. He's not very bright. Ask him."

"About what?" Soraya said. Her jaw was clenched.

"What happened. What his cousin said."

"He told me he can't imagine what his cousin has to hide."

"And the Sutherland?" Felix asked. "There's a reason they've got us up there. What's the next move?"

Franklin sighed. "Stay there," he said. "But you two are both carrying?"

"I think my gun is in my dorm room," Soraya said. "I left it in my other coat."

"I'm carrying the .45," Felix said.

Franklin took two greasy white boxes out of a desk drawer and pushed them across at them.

"Bullets," he said. "We're not targets, but we're in a mess. We have clients. But now we have our own tragedy."

"What's our timing?" Felix asked.

"We've been moving too slow. It's Wednesday. This has to be handled by the end of the weekend. I don't want to go back up to New Hampshire without a bad guy."

"And if we don't have somebody in hand by then, the police are going to make a mess of things," Soraya said. She stood up.

"Thanks," Felix said. Soraya stood away from him, but she seemed to be mirroring his moves. "You know where to find us."

They went out.

14 Philip and Gennardi were in the van in front of the Apple offices on West Fifty-sixth Street.

"He called her?" Philip asked. He was leaned far back in the passenger seat, watching the door. It was five and they were waiting for Simon to come out. Gennardi had talked to Franklin, and they'd decided they just wanted to learn where Stuart and Simon went. See what the father and son did next. Meanwhile, Gennardi had been text-messaging and e-mailing his wife.

"Franklin?"

"No, Daffy Duck. Of course Franklin. Did he call her?"

"Yeah, she says he did."

"He's worried," Philip said. "He couldn't wait for you to take care of it yourself."

"Fuck Franklin, he should worry about his own problems."

"Fuck Franklin," Philip said. "To hell with him." He turned to Gennardi and laughed, and Gennardi laughed back, and they were both deep bass laughs—the sounds of men who hadn't laughed in a long time.

Gennardi said, "The truth is, I breathe easier knowing that he called. Each night I was afraid she'd divorce me. The fact that she took his call means maybe that won't happen."

"It is a relief," Philip said.

"He said she was worried about my gun," Gennardi said.

"Who wouldn't be? Idiot husband puts himself in a cheap hotel, forgets his gun, and the next day somebody gets shot in the alley out back?"

The two men turned to each other and laughed again. But this time the laughter was short.

Then Simon Apple came out of the office building. He turned into the parking lot next door and came out a few minutes later driving a silver BMW SUV. He wore sunglasses. Gennardi had the van running and they pulled out, with a few cars between them. Gennardi relaxed. The traffic was intense.

Felix took Soraya up to her room in McBain. She hadn't been there in days.

"How the fuck am I supposed to study for finals with this shit happening?" she said. She picked up a book from her desk—Luce Irigaray. She dropped it on her bed, sat down next to it, then pushed the book onto the floor, where it landed with a good thump. Felix sat on her desk chair. He said nothing. He thought, There's a murderer out there. We're wasting time.

"We need to get back to that hotel," Soraya said. Her voice was monotone, a woman in a tollbooth giving change. She didn't lie down on her bed. She only sat there, her hands in her lap, her face down. There was a photograph of Gus on Soraya's desk, taken on a night at Eden-Roc. He was smiling, in one of his black suits, looking slightly beyond the camera's eye.

"We should take this," Felix said, and reached for it.

"Give it to me," Soraya said. Felix did, and still she wouldn't let her skin touch his.

"Where's your gun?" Felix asked.

"Not here. Maybe Edwige took it," Soraya said. "She borrows it sometimes."

"For what?"

"When she goes to party up in Inwood. She doesn't load it or anything. It's stupid. Don't ask me about it now."

Soraya rubbed her eyes. Her breathing was uneven.

"I know my father didn't mention it, but will there be funeral arrangements? Do you need help with that?"

Soraya made a sound that was like a laugh. She rubbed her forehead with the flat of her palm.

"Felix," she said, "there isn't going to be any funeral. His mother died of an overdose ten years ago. Father disappeared before that. He's got some relatives in the Bronx with no money and it'd be nothing but a burden on them to force them to claim him. Funerals cost money. Some people just can't afford them. He'll go from the morgue, once the case is closed, to Potter's Field. That'll be the end of him."

"No headstone."

"No."

"Do you want us to help?"

"I don't want you to do shit," she said. "I want to find the guy who did it and end him. That's all I want."

Felix watched her, but she didn't get up from the bed. Around them the dorm was quiet.

"Where's your father buried?"

"Mount Olivet Cemetery," Soraya whispered. "In Queens."

"Let's go there, let's go visit your father." Felix stood up. "We'll go downtown, pick up my car."

"No," Soraya said. She'd drawn her knees up and she was glaring at him.

"We don't have much time."

He waited while she grabbed a few things and put them into a bag. He stood by the door, one hand loose on the gun in his shoulder holster.

Felix drove the Roadrunner slowly over the bumps of the Long Island Expressway. Soraya watched the great mess of Queens, and they didn't speak till they'd arrived at the front entrance to Mount Olivet Cemetery. Soraya sat silently while Felix got directions to Billy Navarro's plot. She had a message on her phone, and she listened to it while Felix spoke with the attendant. When Felix came back, shielding his eyes from the steady wind, Soraya's nose was twitching.

"What?"

"That was Morris Apple. He asked me out for tonight."

"Good," Felix said. "We'll deal with that later. Now we take this path."

They drove for ten minutes before they found it. The grave had a flat stone that had once been white. It said, *William "Billy" Navarro, 1960–1990, Husband, Father, Detective, NYPD.* It was next to several other Navarros.

"My grandparents," Soraya said. "My great-aunt. The rest are in Puerto Rico. Give me a minute."

Felix stepped back to the thin road that had brought them there. They hadn't brought flowers or anything. He shrugged his suit jacket tight around his shoulders and pulled his hat down hard on his head. He leaned against the Roadrunner and put his hands behind him, felt the warmth of the engine.

He watched her as she knelt in front of her father's grave. She put her forehead on the stone and cried. The sobs racked her body, but he knew not to go near her.

It was over in a few minutes. She stood up. Shook out her shoulders. Then she came over to Felix.

"What'd you tell him?" Felix asked as they walked back.

"I apologized," she said, "for falling in love with exactly the kind of man he didn't like. I swore to him I'd never do that again."

Soraya bumped against him and almost stumbled. He grabbed her around the middle, held her up.

"Get off me," she said. But her voice wasn't hard. He held her lightly while she cried.

Franklin sat at Zitto's with Jenny Hurly. They were sharing a very small piece of panna cotta and drinking espresso.

The restaurant wasn't crowded. It was nearly three, and lunch was long over.

"What are you thinking?" Jenny asked. She'd been telling him about a job offer she'd just received, working in the photo department at *Art in America*. She was going to take the job. In a way, they were celebrating. But she was going easy because things were dark around Franklin. And she could see that.

"I'm thinking how this all isn't quite fitting. Should be a simple case. But the sequence isn't right, the style is all wrong. Nobody's acting like they should."

They'd arrived at the last bite of dessert.

"There are too many players," Jenny said.

"How do you know that?" Franklin asked.

"Sequence, pattern. It always falls into place if it's only one person. People don't surprise. It's about finding order. You're annoyed because you can't find order. To me it seems like more than one person did something wrong."

"It's not a shirt," Franklin said. "You don't fit together pieces of fabric and then sew them till it looks right."

Jenny watched him. Her honey brown eyes were soft, but her jaw was set. He knew she didn't want to lose him for another three months to a case, to mourning.

She said, "You know you're wrong. It's exactly the way you described. Once it's done, it will feel all sewn together."

Franklin took a moment before he smiled at her. He kissed her mouth and ran his hand up her thigh. She made a noise in her throat and reached out and rubbed the back of his head. Franklin's phone went off.

"Wait. I gotta take this," Franklin said. Into the phone he said, "Is she okay? You're not letting her out of your sight, are you?"

Then he listened to Felix tell him that Soraya was going to go out with Morris.

Franklin sighed. He stared at Jenny. She was running her finger over the dessert plate, putting the confectioners' sugar on the tip of her tongue.

"Can she handle it?" Franklin asked.

"It's Soraya. She's going to do just fine," Felix said. "But I can't watch them. You can put Philip and Gennardi on it. At the Sutherland, nine tonight."

"Done," Franklin said. He ended the call. To Jenny he said, "I told you about Eitel Vasquez?"

Jenny nodded at him. "Doesn't he have a suspect in custody?" she asked.

"He's got someone he's watching, but they're not in custody. Doesn't matter, really."

"Why not?"

"Because if someone's hiring people, there's a line out the door of dumb heavies who'll do a killing."

"But you should see Vasquez, anyway."

"Yeah. And I have to protect my goddaughter now that her boyfriend got killed right in the middle of my investigation."

"Don't be that way, Franklin," Jenny said. "Don't take blame for things you didn't do. But you should protect her."

"No more talk about what I'm doing wrong," Franklin said. "Let's celebrate your career."

"Do you love me?" Jenny asked.

"Yes, I love you," Franklin said. He took her in his arms and kissed her.

15

Soraya and Felix had been sitting in the suite at the Sutherland since dusk. They'd talked with Franklin and with Philip and Gennardi. Everything was set. Soraya couldn't say for sure where Morris was taking her, but neither the men nor the van had been identified, so they could stay very close. And they would.

"It doesn't have to be tonight," Felix said. Soraya watched him. She was drinking glass after glass of ice water that she poured from a silver pitcher.

"We've got to speed it up. The cops are fucking up the case as we speak. You know that."

"Soraya," Felix said.

"We've been sitting here all afternoon. I'm ready to learn something," she said.

"Okay," Felix said. "But go easy—walk away if there's a problem. If you feel like you can't do it, just walk away."

"Yeah . . ." She trailed off.

They were both seated on one couch, angled toward the window. There was a fiery sunset over Central Park that they were watching.

"I need some rest before I see Morris. I'm just going to sleep for a few hours," Soraya said.

"I can bring you a blanket."

"Thank you."

Felix went into the bedroom and took the blanket from the bed. He got a pillow, too, and came back to the couch. Soraya was lying down now, on her back. She was watching him.

"I don't need the pillow," she said. He dropped it onto the opposite couch. He came and spread the dark blue blanket over her and she closed her eyes. He sat down and she put her head on his thigh, nestled for a moment into his abdomen. She fell asleep before she could start to cry.

Felix looked out the window at the dusk, searched out the spots of yellow from the streetlights that dotted the park. He stroked her cheek with the backs of his fingers and though the room was warm, he didn't fall asleep. He kept one hand on Soraya's sleeping form.

"I appreciate this," Franklin said to Eitel Vasquez. The two men walked with Gennardi into a room at Manhattan Central Booking. The place had recently been painted, and the extra layer of gray paint on the walls seemed to glisten in the fluorescent light.

"Don't think it's a favor," Vasquez said. "It's an exchange of information. I just need a little extra piece of pork before I turn my guy over to the DA."

Franklin glanced at Gennardi. Gennardi shook his head—he knew nothing. And Franklin had no information at all beyond the guess he'd made that morning about Gus Moravia. He had suspicions, but those were just going to annoy Vasquez. But still, he wanted to see the suspect. If the guy was a hired professional or just an unhappy cleaning crew guy—the difference would make itself known in a matter of seconds.

The men walked quietly over the cement floor. Occasionally a cop in uniform would recognize Franklin from the papers and glare, or smile if he was looking for a job and a way out, but otherwise their walk was nothing but long. The only real noise in the corridor came from the two-way radios the DOC officers wore.

"You knock him around a little?" Franklin asked.

"What do you care," Vasquez said.

"I like to know in advance."

Vasquez chewed on that for a moment. He was in a green suit that was too tight over his little shoulders and too baggy around his waist. Franklin thought he looked like a bad elf, but he kept that to himself, too.

"I didn't have to hit him," Vasquez said. "He's got no alibi. He's the killer and he admits it."

"I can't think of a reason to disagree," Franklin said.

Gennardi began to whistle "Greensleeves" and Franklin glared at him.

Vasquez said, "With this guy, you don't need any background—you see him, it says it all."

"It says what?" Franklin asked patiently.

"Laundry room manager. Took shit for too long. Couldn't get to the Apples and loved the staff, so he started taking out guests."

Franklin and Gennardi looked at each other. The story reeked of bullshit and randomness. All it sounded like was what a cop and the newspapers would want to believe.

They stopped in front of a small gray cell that looked like a lot of other small gray cells that were lined up on the north wall of the facility. There were some federal prisoners in the cells, too, suspected terrorists and Mexican drug dealers, so federal guards were standing around. But in front of their cell there was only a lone city cop in a baggy blue windbreaker, reading a copy of *The Onion* and laughing into his fist.

"He's been crying," the cop said, and reached out with his left hand to open the door without getting up from his chair.

"About what?" Franklin asked.

"How the fuck should I know?" the cop said. He licked his right thumb and turned a page of the newspaper. Franklin glanced at the headline: AREA MAN TURNS STRANGER INTO UNWILLING FRIEND. They went in.

"Miguel Santorez," Eitel said. The room had a barred window, several metal folding chairs, and a steel table. There was a black rubber garbage can next to the door, and that was it.

"I didn't even ask for a lawyer yet," Miguel said.

"That was stupid," Franklin said.

He sat down across from Miguel and looked at him. The guy was forty and thin, with four days of beard growth over a sallow face that wouldn't have looked out of place on a flea-bitten Central Park carriage horse. Thick red lips and deep-set, watery black eyes.

"What do you want to ask me?" Miguel asked. Vasquez muttered something Franklin didn't bother to hear.

"You committed three murders or four?"

"I'm not going to say about that."

Franklin sat back. He watched Miguel Santorez and worked to think about anything else, knowing the scowl on his face would make up the difference. Jenny Hurly had made him buy new shoes, Mephistos, and they were black and a little streamlined for his tastes, but did he really give a shit? They were the most expensive shoes he'd ever had in his life, but he had the money, didn't he? And hadn't it made Jenny happy when he'd thrown away his black clodhoppers from Dave's Army & Navy and put on the Mephistos?

"Okay, okay," Miguel said. "I'm not going to say about what I did do and did not do, but I'm responsible for everything I did. I take full responsibility. We go to trial, it's all about me."

"You got a wife," Franklin said.

Miguel nodded. He kept testing the top of his mouth with his tongue, and it was contorting his facial expressions so they wouldn't match up with what he was thinking. A trick, Franklin knew, that someone must've taught him when he'd done time before.

"And you got some kids, up there in El Barrio?"

Again Miguel nodded. Now he was biting the insides of his lips. The room was dead quiet.

"Show me how you hold a knife," Franklin said.

Miguel shook his head, said, "Uh-uh."

"Even to cut meat?"

"Nope."

"Show me your hands."

Miguel held out his hands. He had long fingers and his palms were nearly devoid of lines. Franklin reached out and touched them, pressed his thumbs into the center of Miguel's palm. They were hard and fleshy, with an overcoat of thick skin.

"Washed a lot of clothes for the Apples," Miguel said.

"Never made much money," Franklin said.

"Not much. But I was always—" Miguel cut himself off.

"A hard worker," Franklin said. Miguel glared at him, and slowly Franklin stood up. He put his hands on the table and stared down at Miguel Santorez.

Franklin said, "We'll see how it shakes out. If you're lucky, you'll get paid by whoever you're protecting before we catch them. You can give that money to your family before you get arrested for conspiracy."

Before he went out, Franklin took a quick look back at Miguel Santorez. The man was biting his cheeks to keep from crying. The cop locked the door behind them.

"Now you share with me," Vasquez said when they'd made it back to reception.

"Why, I got nothing," Franklin said. "I didn't learn anything in there."

"We'll revisit Santorez," Vasquez said. "What I want to know comes from the outside. Now share."

Franklin looked at Gennardi, who had found something interesting to stare at farther down the hall.

"There's something about the Apples that isn't right," Franklin said. "And that's all I'm giving you for now."

"What about my guy?"

"What about him—you think that guy committed three or four murders?"

"Anyone is capable of it," Vasquez said, and smiled at Franklin.

"Ease off," Gennardi said, but Vasquez and Franklin ignored him. Then, because he had so little to offer, Franklin decided to play it another way.

"That's where you're wrong," Franklin said. "The psych guy they brought in to tell you that was smoking evidence. Because not everyone is capable of it. I know what you think of me and I don't care. But don't let it cloud your head. That guy is no murderer. He's a disgruntled employee. Say it a million times, it doesn't equal killer. You're wasting your time. Let him go."

Vasquez had already turned around. He was walking back down the corridor toward his suspect.

He called over his shoulder, "Until you deliver something better and make us all happy, that's my man down there. And don't come up with some complicated shit, either. Because this guy made it simple. No reason for you to muck it up."

Franklin and Gennardi didn't stare after him. They turned and walked toward the street exit. Outside it was dark, and because they were in Chinatown, they started heading toward Joe's Shanghai on Pell Street for a takeout box of soup dumplings.

"Detective Vasquez really likes you," Gennardi said.

"Ultimately, our friend Eitel acts like an honest cop," Franklin said. "But at its base, what I just said seems to contradict his misguided desire to railroad a dingdong."

"Let's take our dumplings to Garibaldi's and have a drink," Gennardi said. "Then we can unpack what you just said."

*   *   *

Late on Wednesday night Soraya stood with Morris Apple on Sixth Avenue, just above Houston Street, in front of Bar Pitti.

"I thought maybe you wouldn't want to come out tonight," Morris said. Soraya smiled at him. He wore an orange corduroy suit and New Balance running sneakers. He had a purple scarf around his neck that mostly covered his herringbone-patterned blue shirt. She watched as he casually leaned against a tree. The bald-headed host came out and swore up and down it'd only be one more minute, one more minute or less for Mr. Morris Apple.

"No rush," Morris said. "It's a beautiful night."

Sweet fat boy, she thought. Sweet, ineffectual fat boy. Soraya watched him. She set her shoulders. She looked down at her nails, at her boots, tried to cast her eyes anywhere that would ensure that she thought about nothing. She would be a receptacle for information, that was all.

"Why wouldn't I want to come out?" Soraya asked.

She smiled at him. She thought his voice was like an old woman's. He smiled and his lips were thin in his round face, revealing pointed teeth that were oddly spaced. Considering all his money, she couldn't understand why he didn't fix them.

"Because of what happened to your friend," Morris said.

"What friend?"

"Gus Moravia, the man who was murdered downtown last night."

She swayed slightly and was lucky to find the cold iron of the back of a bench behind her. She leaned against it, tried to focus on the traffic that roared up Sixth. She looked quickly at him and found that she couldn't find his hands, that he'd slipped them into the pockets of his coat. He stepped toward her then. Before she could help it, she'd glared at him. He receded.

She said, "How did you know he was my friend?"

"I think it was my cousin who mentioned it, actually. But he wouldn't say more about you. He's very tight-lipped, my cousin."

"You two don't have much in common, do you?" she asked. "It's like what you were saying the other night—you often seem perplexed by him."

"The other night was about me. Let's let tonight be about you," Morris said.

Soraya only shook her head. She said, "I am sad about Gus, but when you called, I couldn't imagine a better way to spend an evening than with a new friend like you."

He smiled at her. His lips were dry and cracked and his pupils seemed nearly black behind his plastic-framed glasses. She smiled at him and he seemed to like that very much.

"We didn't have to wait long at all," Morris said as the smiling host came running out toward them.

"It's in a family that it happens," Gennardi said. He'd been chewing on a toothpick, and he took it out of his mouth and gestured with it before breaking it in two.

"How's that?" Philip asked. They watched the BMW 745 sedan that had settled in front of Bar Pitti. They could see into the restaurant to where Soraya sat with Morris.

"You didn't listen the first time," Gennardi said. "Let me tell you the story of some rats who lived in a house near mine when I was growing up."

"Do I have to come back with a nursery story of my own? From my country?" Philip laughed.

"You don't have to come back with shit. I'm telling you a story."

"Okay," Philip said.

Gennardi said, "These were a family of rats, and they

kept squabbling with each other. It was all about This is my cheese, you ate my cheese, who moved my cheese, like that."

Philip nodded. He said, "They were hungry."

"That's right. Exactly. They were hungry. So they come to a house. Only it's not that big. So one of the rats, King Rat, goes running into the house and he starts eating. The other rats are outside, and they watch."

"They can't fit in." Philip yawned. He wore black leather driving gloves and he covered his mouth. It looked like Morris had ordered a bottle of wine. They watched him examine the label.

"Right. So this one greedy rat eats and eats and pretty soon he's eating away at the insides of the house. So his family gets bored and they leave him there. They go to the beach."

"Rat Beach on Coney Island."

"There. Meanwhile this rat, he's eaten the whole inner structure of the house and he's fat as fuck. Next thing he knows, the house collapses around him. And he's naked and fat and unprotected. He's scared out of his mind."

"He doesn't know which way is the beach."

"And it's all because he was greedy."

Philip sighed. He watched Morris taste the wine and nod. "We have the same story in Zimbabwe. Only the rats were the Rhodesians. And the house was our farmland. You read it somewhere, figure it relates to your situation?"

"My situation? I was talking about the Apples. The problem with me is that I went elsewhere, I thought I could get better cheese—oh, God. I'm sorry I put it that way."

Philip got out his pair of Newcon optics and trained them on the windows of the restaurant. He could see Soraya grip the legs of her chair, as if she were holding steady against a strong wind. Then she stood up. Dinner was over.

"Why'd you do it?" Philip said. He keyed the ignition as the lights went on inside the BMW.

"Hard to say," Gennardi said. "I guess I just got to drinking one night and I forgot what makes me happy."

"You say that to her?" Philip asked as he pulled into traffic.

"No," Gennardi said. He was getting on the phone to Felix.

"You could try it," Philip said. "It's better than the rat story."

Morris and Soraya drove uptown, to a town house on East Sixty-third near the park. They went in and there was one servant, an owlish-looking man who wasn't yet forty.

"Excuse me for a moment, won't you?" Morris said. He went down the corridor and into a room on his left, beneath the staircase. She imagined it was a bathroom. The servant took her coat.

She said, "Thanks. It's a nice evening, isn't it?"

The man nodded. He seemed to be trembling slightly, and that was when she realized that the foyer was terribly cold.

"Almost warmer in the streets," she said. "If I start screaming, you'll know I'm freezing my ass off and you can come running with a baseball bat and a hot water bottle."

"Yes, ma'am," the servant said. Though he didn't smile, his eyes flickered at her. And she thought that was probably enough. He'd remember her.

"It was a joke," Soraya said.

A door opened on her left, and Morris's face appeared. The room was dark behind him.

"Come in here."

The room was massive. A three-log fire burned brightly in the fireplace and that provided most of the light. There was a great bay window that looked out into the street, but wooden shutters covered the panes. She could just see carpets on the floor and three groupings of furniture: by the windows, the fireplace, and then farther back, toward pocket doors that must lead to a dining room. The fire crackled and spat, and Soraya found herself looking at it, drawn to it.

Morris walked her to the area in front of the fireplace, but he didn't sit down, and so she didn't, either. She could see paintings on the walls, too, what might have been old masters. A study of a young girl playing on the floor in front of her mother was certainly a Sargent and nearly priceless. She twitched her nose.

"It's a wonderful fire," she said.

"Yes. I have one built every night. My mother spent most of her time in this room before she died," Morris said. "She made sure it was kept very warm."

He sat down on a deep red couch and clasped his hands together between his knees. He coughed slightly and looked down at his shoes. Slowly Soraya sat across from him on a wooden daybed with gnarled legs and a tooled leather cushion that was about as soft as a bench in the subway.

She said, "I'm sorry. I didn't know about your mother."

He said, "I know this evening was supposed to be fun."

"No, no," Soraya said. "I'm happy to just sit here for a while with you." She wondered if the servant was going to come and bring them something to drink. But then she realized it didn't matter. She wouldn't drink or eat anything that came out of this house.

"You live alone here?" Soraya asked.

"Since my mother left, about four years ago. She died soon after that."

Which would've made him twenty, Soraya thought. He'd been left alone? His cousin and uncle hadn't invited him to live with them?

"And your father died."

"When I was four," Morris said.

"My father died, too," Soraya said.

"It sort of weakens your respect for life, when a parent dies so young."

"Yes, I suppose it does," Soraya said.

Neither of them spoke for a few minutes. They watched the fire. Soraya felt somehow beholden to the gloom. She wasn't sure if Morris was out of his mind, but she was somehow charmed by his sadness, by his willingness to spend his youth in a darkened parlor room, watching a fire that had been built for his mother, who was long dead. It was creepy, sure, but she'd never seen anything like it, and it interested her. Or perhaps it was simply the warmth and her need to relax after what had been not the worst day of her life, but one of them. One of several unbelievably horrible days.

She looked up and saw that Morris hadn't inched closer to her but had moved away, to a patterned chair off to the right. He gazed at her.

"I thought a private meeting would be easier," Morris said. "You see, I need your help."

"I don't understand," Soraya said. "But if I can help you, I will." She felt something beyond simply being tired. She realized that she'd have to listen carefully.

"You don't get a lot of sympathy," he said. He was clenching and unclenching his fat little fingers. He stood up suddenly. There was a glass carafe of wine on the sideboard. Morris poured a glass for each of them. Soraya put the glass to her closed lips, put it down.

"I don't?" Soraya asked.

"No. I meant when you're me. When you have so much money, it makes people blind to everything else."

"That's a pity," Soraya said, and yawned.

"I never said that my uncle killed my father," Morris said. "And I did not say that my uncle had my mother murdered."

"No?" Soraya asked.

"But just because I didn't say those things aloud—you can imagine that I might think them sometimes, and that might make me afraid for my own life. You can imagine how I might feel."

"I can't," Soraya said. "Tell me."

"You see, I'm next."

"They've hired someone to kill you?" Soraya asked.

Morris went and stood by the fireplace. He took an iron from a stand and poked at the burning logs. Soraya watched his movements. They were mincing and soft. He was being terribly careful with the iron. He seemed almost afraid to upset the balance of the logs that had undoubtedly been set in place by his servant.

"No," Morris said. "They hired someone to kill those women from Texas and the others. They'll kill me themselves."

"Please," Soraya said. "Explain what you mean."

"They can't—" Morris paused. He put the tips of his fingers to his lips. "It's not simple, you see. They can't just kill me, the way they killed my father. They'd bring holy hell down on themselves if they did that. So what I imagine is that they're going to try to place all these killings on me. They're spinning a web. And then once they've got it nice and tight, they'll do something really horrible. Arrange my suicide or something. It'll be tied together then, and they'll be all set. Everything will belong to them."

"You really believe that?" Soraya asked.

"I shouldn't say 'they,'" Morris said. He appeared not to have heard her. "I should say 'he.' Simon's planned all this out. I don't know who he hired, but he hired someone. That someone is coming to get me."

Soraya finished her glass of wine.

She said, "Please sit down. You're making me uncomfortable."

"I don't know why he had Gus Moravia killed last night. But I'm sure he did."

"What do you want me to do?" she asked.

"I want you to make a lot of noise about them. I think they killed your boyfriend. I'll help you in any way I can. But you've got to hurry. Before they kill me."

"Thanks for the drink," Soraya said. She stood up.

"Please stay," Morris said. "I hate being alone here."

He reached out to her then and tried to take her hand. But she stepped back.

"It's very difficult for me to touch anyone just now." But she knew it wasn't true. After all, she'd slept with her head in Felix's lap that very afternoon.

"Anyway, you'll be okay. You're alone here all the time." She took one last look at the ancient room and walked into the hallway. The owlish servant appeared there and handed over her coat.

"Do you believe me?" Morris asked.

"I'll do what I can for you."

16

She went out the door and turned left, walked toward the park. A van followed her. Two blocks south of Morris's house, on Fifth Avenue, the van stopped and Philip pulled her inside.

"Let's get down to Franklin's," Gennardi said. "You have something?"

"I think so," Soraya said. "But hurry. I'm so tired."

It was just past ten, and the trip from the East Sixties down to Franklin's office in the flower district took no time at all. Philip and Gennardi were quiet. Soraya struggled to think of anything else to say to them, to keep them from saying they were sorry about Gus.

"Philip, I heard they finally took Mugabe out of power. Apparently his deputies had been disappearing for weeks. Did you have a hand in any of that?"

"Oh, Soraya," Philip said. "You know I can't talk about my freelance work."

"Government contracts could help Franklin's business quite a lot," Soraya said. "And it doesn't matter which government."

"Well, you have to have the right kind of look to do good work in Africa," Philip said. "Though we might be able to slip you in through some kind of student visa. I'll look into it, if you're serious."

Philip stroked the Desert Eagle handgun that rested on the side of his rib cage. "In any case, let's take care of this business first."

They drove in silence along Central Park South. Though the day had been somewhat warm, the night was cold. And Soraya shivered. She wondered how many days she had in her before she fell apart. Three seemed like too many. Perhaps two.

"We're not going up with you," Gennardi said when they'd arrived. "Felix is there. We're going to keep watching Simon."

"Where is he?" Soraya asked.

"He works late," Gennardi said. "Then he goes to see his friends at Au Bar, mostly. He keeps his car parked outside. It gets ticketed. He doesn't care."

"What about his father?"

"He's home in bed by ten every night. A town house on Sutton Place. Looks like it was built by the Addams family."

"It kind of was," Soraya said. "Thank you. Thank you for keeping me safe."

She went upstairs. Philip and Gennardi watched her go.

Gennardi said, "I wonder how long till she falls apart."

"If you'll listen, I think I can explain the whole thing," Soraya said when she'd gotten into Franklin's office and sat down with Felix.

"Five minutes," Franklin said. "Then Felix takes you back to the hotel."

Soraya said, "He's like something endangered, some kind of weak animal."

"Morris is?" Felix asked.

"He thinks Simon is trying to kill him. We know that Stuart Apple killed Morris's father, Max. Right?" Soraya asked.

Franklin and Felix said nothing. They were drinking short glasses of scotch.

"Simon is looking to destroy Morris. But he can't do it outright. First he kills some guests, then he tries to pin it on Morris. It isn't easy, but it's the only way. It follows—if Simon and his father can get rid of Morris, they'll be twice as rich. And that's all anybody in that family ever wanted, except Morris."

"Why would Morris tell you all this?" Felix asked.

"To get back at Stuart Apple," Soraya said. "For killing his parents. He hasn't said that. But I suspect it. I know what it's like to lose your father. I can feel what he's feeling."

"What's that?" Felix asked, but his voice was soft.

"He's lonely. And he's afraid. I'm sure Simon asked Gus to kill someone, and Gus said no, so Simon had him killed. Did Simon ask Gus to kill Morris? Maybe."

"So we're looking for a thin man who was hired by Simon and Stuart Apple," Franklin said.

Soraya nodded.

"Let's get you to bed," Felix said.

"Think on what I've said. I'm more right than anyone else, and now I'm closer to this, too."

For a while no one said anything. Felix sipped his scotch.

Then Franklin said, "There's a man in custody. But he won't say who hired him or if anyone did. We can wait through the night. His real story will come tumbling out."

Soraya only nodded, acquiesced. She and Felix got up and went out.

Franklin sat in his office. He'd just gotten a baseball cap with a silver *W* on it, a gift from the old boys he used to work for down at Wackenhut. He hadn't heard from them in five years. He knew what it meant: they'd given him the Texas cousins and they expected him to deliver. It was all legal contracts with those boys. They sealed deals in whispers. Then they typed them up and had lawyers go over them. When he'd left them to come back to New York, they'd agreed to let him go, provided that he be available to them for certain necessary services. Now they'd delivered these two widowers from Texas and they expected results. And he needed to figure out a way to provide them.

The phone rang. He glanced at the caller ID. The number came up blocked. He watched it for a few moments before he picked it up.

"Franklin Novak? I'm glad I caught you. This is Stuart Apple. We haven't spoken since these new developments. Why don't you come by first thing in the morning and we can talk? Your boy and his friend, they're still at the Sutherland, I hope?" Stuart Apple spoke in a long whisper.

Franklin said nothing. He settled the cap on his bald head, pulled the brim down. He thought that things that seem conspiratorial rarely are. He told himself that.

"Tomorrow morning, then," Franklin said. "We'll be in to see you at ten."

Franklin went and met Jenny Hurly for dinner at Zitto's. He walked in and refused to even so much as look at Karen, though he didn't feel terrific about being judgmental. He just didn't feel big enough to act otherwise. Karen stood at the bar, looking utterly forlorn. The black bow tie she wore was rumpled and at an angle.

He sat down across from Jenny Hurly. She wore a black suit and a cream-colored scarf. She was drinking a reddish-colored cocktail that had been served in a martini glass. Franklin had no idea what it was.

"You're early," Franklin said. She smiled at him.

"My first day on the job. The editor in chief kept us there till just now," Jenny said. "I feel lucky I got here at all."

Richard came and stood by them. "Hello, Jenny. Let me tell you the specials."

When he was done, Franklin said, "To her, you talk."

Richard only glanced down at him, said nothing. When he was gone, Franklin said, "He's lucky he knows what I like to eat; otherwise we'd really have a problem."

"I saw you glare at Karen on the way in," Jenny said. "Why?"

Franklin picked up a piece of bread and dabbed it in the plate of olive oil. He ate and with his mouth full said, "She was the one. You remember I told you about Gennardi's affair? It was her that fucked up his marriage."

"Hey," Jenny said. "Just because you ended up on the wrong end of adultery, that doesn't mean you have the right to be the judge and the jury."

Franklin stopped chewing. He stared at her.

"I'm serious," Jenny said. "Don't legislate other people's happiness. You should know better. I've been listening to you be upset about Gennardi's problems for days and said nothing, but when I saw you just now, how you glared at that woman, that was wrong."

"That's why I love you," Franklin said. "Because you see things. I had no idea it was because of what happened to me that I've been trying to fix what's the matter with them."

"I hope that's not the only reason."

"No, no, of course not," Franklin said. "It's more complex than that." He smiled and felt young.

Richard came to the table with a bottle of Barolo that Franklin liked. He poured out two glasses. Another waiter delivered plates of *spinaci saltati.* Great chunks of garlic rested in the middle of the spinach and looked like golden eggs.

17

Franklin stood in front of his closet on Thursday morning. He was out of shirts.

Jenny had already left to go back to her own apartment before work, so Franklin's bedroom was quiet. He could hear his own breathing, see the movement of his gut as he stared at the row of naked wire hangers. There was his pile of a dozen gray and white shirts in a heap on the floor.

He had a system, a habit of wearing essentially the same thing again and again. Once every two weeks he brought the shirts down to be cleaned. And now he'd run out. He shook his head and grabbed a Police Athletic League sweatshirt off a shelf.

He heard his cell phone ringing and went out to the living room, where he'd left his overcoat on the couch. He wrestled the phone out of the pocket.

"We let Miguel go," Eitel Vasquez said.

"You didn't keep him for all seventy-two hours?"

"Nah. We wanted to see what he'd do. He wasn't the killer. You knew that."

"He said he was." Franklin squinted in the blast of sun coming through his windows.

"Money talks," Eitel said. "We need a killer. If it's got to be complicated, so be it. What happened wasn't street. I'm beginning to understand that."

"Then why'd your guy confess? Because you hit him?"

"Nah. He's hiding from something. We're not sure what it is."

"I'll let you know when I think of something smart to say," Franklin said.

"You have our cooperation," Vasquez said.

"What changed?"

"I'm not going to lose my job over some rich boy's spat is what changed," Vasquez said, and hung up.

Franklin put the phone down. So, he thought, they'd beaten the Miguel character till he'd admitted he'd been paid to take a fall. But whatever Miguel had said, it hadn't been enough to start arresting people who could afford good lawyers. Franklin frowned. So now he was the one who was supposed to do the real work.

He walked into the bedroom. He glanced at the top of his dresser and saw a pile of neatly stacked shirts. There were four, and each was brightly colored, with a soft pattern. He picked them up. He rubbed the fabric with his thumb. A gift from Jenny.

He slowly buttoned a bottle green shirt with a spread collar over his undershirt and looked at his reflection in the bathroom mirror. His bald head. The deep folds of skin that extended from his nostrils to mouth. He went through what Soraya had learned, let the logic swirl around him. There were three Apples. The Apples didn't like to share. So one or two Apples were lying and trying to wrestle all of the Apple properties away from the other one. Legal explorations had failed. So one or two Apples were setting up another one to take the fall. It might work. Then an Apple would go away to jail, perhaps even get his life ended if the right DA took the case. He decided that was his bet, that Soraya was calling it right.

He called Gennardi and Philip and told them to go back through all of the public records relating to ownership of all the Apple buildings. He couldn't help thinking they must've missed something. Then his phone rang again. It was Ed Wallingford.

Franklin met Felix in the little park in front of the Plaza hotel at a quarter to ten. The sun was terribly bright and they stood surrounded by pigeons, who were eating food left by the tourists.

"Our clients called this morning," Franklin said. "They're restless. They want to go home."

"We only need a few more days," Felix said.

"And Eitel Vasquez released his prisoner," Franklin said.

"Which is no surprise," Felix said. "I've been thinking about all this. I'm not sure that Soraya's right, that it's Simon. But I know one thing."

"An Apple is lying," Franklin said.

"That's right. An Apple is . . . ," Felix said.

"No longer fresh," Franklin said. "Rotten. Has a worm in it. Enough. How is Soraya?"

"I fell asleep on the couch while she was watching TV. She watched all night. I think she might have called one of those shopping channels and ordered a gold bracelet or something. Or maybe I dreamed that."

"Where is she now?"

"She went to school. She's seeing Edwige. I'm going to stay with her in her dorm room tonight. She doesn't want to be in the Sutherland anymore."

"Of course. Do you know if she spoke to her mother?"

"She did," Felix said. "But she didn't tell her the whole story—only about Gus dying. Let's go."

Franklin glanced over at his son. But Felix was staring straight ahead. His suit was cleaned and pressed. His long hair was combed and tucked behind his ears. Pleasant surprise, Franklin thought. Unexpected cleanliness.

"Nice shirt," Felix said.

They went into the foyer and said hello to Joanne Gordimer, who looked like she hadn't slept in days. She moved slowly, and when she went down the hall to see if

Stuart was ready, she bumped into the wall and nearly upset a framed photograph of a totally nondescript building the Apples owned on East Thirty-sixth Street and Third Avenue.

"Pills," Felix whispered.

"Fear," Franklin whispered back.

"You can go right in," she called out. She yanked a door open on the right, staggered through it, and disappeared.

Felix and Franklin went into Stuart Apple's office and sat down. The old man was in there alone. A paper cup filled with steaming coffee was on his desk. He stood up and shook hands with both men. The metal folding chair Simon had used was folded and leaning against one wall. The room smelled dusty and underused, as if Stuart Apple only took his meetings here and did real business elsewhere.

"Gentlemen," Stuart Apple said. He unbuttoned his suit coat and sat back down at his desk. "I've called you here because I want to help in any way that I can. The police are restless. Vacancy rates in my hotels are skyrocketing. I can see that we're running out of time."

"How can you help?" Franklin asked. The old man was shaking slightly, a tremor beneath his jaw, the result of a twitch that might've begun at the base of his spine.

"This situation sickens me," Stuart Apple said, as if he hadn't heard Franklin speak.

"We're very sorry about it, too," Felix said. "We'd like to see this killer stopped before he strikes again."

Franklin looked over at Felix. The kid was doing something he hadn't seen him do before. And it got his full attention. He was focused and intent. He was getting across one single feeling: How can we help? Franklin had to struggle to keep his mouth shut. Felix was playing Stuart Apple, inasmuch as the old boy could be played. Felix actually looked like a sympathetic listener.

Felix said, "Do you think someone might want to have an adverse effect on your business? Do you think that's what this is about?"

Franklin looked and again, Felix turned on the concern. Stuart seemed to shy away from Felix's act.

Stuart sipped his coffee. He made what little there was of his thin lips disappear completely. He looked at a point between Felix and Franklin, and his gray eyes didn't waver.

"Take your time," Felix said. "Think about it."

"Though it sickens me beyond the scope of anything that I've ever experienced, I believe it's my nephew, Morris, who's behind this unfortunate series of events. I can't imagine anybody else having this level of access, this level of understanding of what might bring my organization to its knees. He resents me and he always has, ever since his father died in that boating accident and his mother fled Manhattan."

Stuart stopped. He finished his coffee and slid the empty cup slowly to the right until it fell off his desk and landed with a muted pop in a tin garbage can. Then he began again.

"He's just been sitting in his town house, plotting my demise. And of course he'd like to take my son down with me. I'm disgusted with this—of course you can have no idea how awful I feel. But there it is. I've told you. Morris seems to have hired someone to kill the occupants of Apple properties. The killing will stop when we sign the property over to him, which we will not do. Instead we want him put in jail."

After he was finished, no one spoke. Stuart gulped air. He pressed a button on his desk and said, "Joanne, water for all of us."

"But Morris hasn't actually said that," Felix said.

"No," Stuart said. "Not yet."

"Your next appointment is here," Joanne said. Franklin thought she might as well have been reading off a cue card.

"What?" Stuart said. He slowly raised a hand and tried to do a convincing job of mopping his brow. "Well, make them wait. We need another few minutes in here."

"Of course you can imagine our next question," Felix said. Franklin got ready to interrupt, to smooth over what he was sure would be his son's disdain for the Apple's calculated story. But then he saw that Felix wasn't about to say anything. He only stared at the old man.

Stuart said, "Why didn't I mention this possibility when you first came to see me, a week ago?"

"Yes," Felix said.

"I prayed it wasn't true then. Simon and I were in agreement. That though it was entirely possible, it could not be so. We prayed it was a simple jewelry robbery, even though the killer's knowledge of our hotel and his on-tape rambles about that being his first time—these things pointed in another direction."

"So you've changed your minds," Felix said. "You brought us here to tell us this. And what you're saying, in effect, is that we should detain your nephew or have the police arrest him on the grounds that he's responsible for five murders?"

"Yes," Stuart said. "But I'd rather you handled the police and left me out of it. That's why I came to you." The noises he made were quieter than the sound of a Kleenex being pulled from its box. Franklin watched Felix. Franklin thought, Throw him off his game now. See what he does.

"Where is Simon?" Felix asked.

There was a slight flicker in Stuart's eyes. The consideration, Franklin suspected, was whether to answer this question at all. Stuart had already done his work. He probably didn't feel he had to share more.

"I suppose he's working. We're considering remodeling the Sutherland. He's probably over there, consulting with the company that does our interiors. He's good at that sort of thing. We're working hard to salvage what we have. We will fight this current situation. We haven't been in business this long for nothing, you know."

Stuart stood up. His cheeks weren't red. His brow wasn't furrowed.

"Gentlemen, I'm so sorry, but I have to call in my next appointment. Anyway, there it is. You can imagine the moral implication of all I've just said, the pain it gives me."

"Yes, of course," Felix said. "We'll see ourselves out."

They went down the corridor and out the door. They passed no one, not Joanne Gordimer or anyone who might be Stuart Apple's next appointment.

On the street Franklin and Felix began to walk east. Though it was cold and a brittle wind came rolling from the west, the day was still unbelievably bright. The two men walked quickly. Franklin dug a toothpick from the pocket of his coat. Then he found another one and handed it to Felix. They kept walking.

Franklin said, "Call Soraya."

While Felix called, Franklin called Philip and Gennardi. They were still combing through deeds at the municipal real estate bureau downtown.

"It's like we said before. Everything is in trusts," Philip said. "They're a privately held corporation. The distribution of funds isn't public information."

"But a lawyer must've drawn up agreements between all the parties," Franklin said.

"It's Forrest, Greenberg, and Grand-Jean," Philip said. "A man there named Mordechai Goodwin did all the work."

"Talk to him. Then meet me at the office," Franklin said. He glanced at Felix, who had finished his call. He said, "She's all right?"

But Felix was gray.

"No. She left me a message, said she was going to talk to a maid. I called, but I couldn't reach her."

"Let's go," Franklin said. They jumped in a cab. The cabdriver was eating food from McDonald's and the cab reeked of it.

While he rolled down his window, Felix said, "It's a hundred to you if you can get us to Seventy-fifth and Madison in two minutes."

"A thousand wouldn't make it happen," the cabdriver said, with his mouth full of fries.

"We have guns," Franklin said, and showed the driver one. The man set his Big Mac down and sped up.

"I think Soraya was right all along," Felix said. "Simon is setting up his cousin and it's working. He's got his father believing it or in on it, doesn't matter—and now he's going to clean up. Redo the fucking carpets up there and run things his way, the arrogant bastard."

"We can't even detain him," Franklin said. "Not yet."

"Speed it up," Felix said to the driver.

They got going fast on Park Avenue, and the dappled sunlight from the trees on the median flickered over them. There was a full minute where they could do nothing but wait.

"I thought you handled that meeting pretty good," Franklin said. "Seems to me you're listening more carefully these days. And that open-faced look. Where the hell did you pick that up?"

"I owe that and a lot more to Soraya," Felix said simply. "I've been a top-grade asshole ever since I blew into town. I'm beginning to see that. Let us out here."

The cab had come to a stop at East Seventy-fourth. Franklin threw a hundred-dollar bill at the driver, and they got out and ran toward the Sutherland. Neither would say what was disturbing them both. That Soraya had taken in a lot of information firsthand. That she could cause real trouble in court and someone might want to stop her from making it there.

They blew by the doorman. Felix punched the button for the elevator. Then he ran into the Lido. Several women stood there, all perfectly dressed. They were leaning over blueprints and they had swatches of colors and fabrics in their hands.

"Where is Simon Apple?" Felix yelled.

"You missed him," one woman said. "He just left. Could you tell him that we're thinking of jade for the—"

But Felix was running into the elevator that Franklin was holding for him. Franklin shook his head.

Felix said, "I don't like this." He pulled his gun from his shoulder holster and held it low so it wouldn't be immediately visible. Franklin took his gun out, too. He had the new Magnum with him. It looked like he was gripping a foot of silver pipe.

The door to the suite was open and they ran in. Soraya was there. She was bent over a maid, who was short and quite round. The maid was splayed out on the floor, with her dress surrounding her like a ballerina's in *Swan Lake.* She was rocking back and forth. Soraya looked up at the Novaks.

"She was cleaning the room. Somebody came in here and threw her against the wall. They punched her and she blacked out. Then they ripped through all our stuff. My shearling coat is missing. My gun was in that coat. Edwige never had it."

"She won't say who it was?" Felix asked.

"*Quién estuvo?*" Soraya asked.

"*Un gringo,*" the maid said. She went on in Spanish, "How am I supposed to tell the difference? All young white men look the same to me. Weak hair, angry face, dark clothes that cost too much money. All the same."

The maid became hysterical. She pulled up her skirt and pressed it over her face and wouldn't speak. Soraya got up and went to the kitchen to get her a glass of water.

"This is a waste of time," Soraya said. "She says it might as well have been Felix for all she knows."

The maid suddenly stood up and walked out, leaving her cleaning supplies behind her. Soraya followed her into the hall.

"I'm not saying anything about anybody else," the maid said. "You leave me alone."

Felix took a deep breath. Slowly he holstered his gun. "The thing is playing out pretty clear, wouldn't you say? Simon's trying to cover his tracks."

Franklin sat down on one of the pink couches. He grabbed a silk pillow and mopped his sweating skull with it, and then he threw it down. Soraya came back in. She picked her bag up from the floor and frowned.

Franklin said, "I can't say it's clear, no. But no matter what, we're going to find out who killed Gus. We owe you that much, Soraya."

"Bringing Simon down is just the beginning," Felix said. "We swear to you."

Soraya went and stood with her back against the cold window so that she was silhouetted against the midday light. She folded her arms across her chest and shuddered.

"The answer comes when we discover which Apple is lying," Soraya said. "And right now I think I've done a pretty good job of proving that Simon is our liar."

"You think he's making his father back up his story?" Felix asked Franklin.

"I'm not ready to say how they fixed it between them," Franklin said. "But one way or another, it does seem like it's them against Morris."

18

"Do you remember when you last had your gun?" Felix asked Soraya.

Soraya shook her head no. All she said was, "I need some time to myself, away from all this."

They were up in her dorm room and he was waiting for Gennardi and Philip to pick him up. Soraya was slowly going through her bag. The box of bullets Franklin had given her was in there.

"I understand that," Felix said. "But it's not a good time for you to be alone."

Soraya looked over at him. He stood in the door frame, rocking on his heels, watching the window, ready if someone came through the door. She knew he'd be ferocious if anyone came after her. But it wasn't what she liked about him. And she didn't want anyone trying to take care of her.

Soraya shook her head again. She said, "I'm going to spend the day with Edwige. She's got several cans of mace and a very loud voice."

"Don't be funny," Felix said.

"Don't tell me what to do," Soraya said, fast. "Gus is dead. And we don't know who did it. Is he dead because Franklin took on a client? I'm not so sure. Maybe he'd be dead, anyway. Don't tie it all so tight, Felix. There's no reason to."

"Look, somewhere in here, somebody decided that we're going to screw up their plan, and they want us out of the way. We can't have that happen."

"So why don't I worry about me and you worry about you?" Soraya asked. "Franklin only really needs one of us, anyway. And you're preferable. You're his son."

"If they come after me, I'm carrying. And I'm going to stick with Gennardi and Philip. See? I can admit that I'm vulnerable."

"Let's not get into an argument about that," Soraya said. She gave him a tired smile.

"We don't have it together yet, but we're close. We're going after Simon. He'll give up the plan and the thin man. I want you with me or I want you armed. Either take mine or come with me downtown."

"What'd Franklin say?"

"We've got the rest of the day. Tomorrow morning we'll go back up to New Hampshire, check in with the client. They say they want to talk."

There was a knock on the door. Soraya breathed in.

"Hello," she said through the closed door.

"Since when do you keep the door locked?" someone called out. Soraya opened the door. It was Edwige. She wasn't smiling. She had a copy of the *Spectator* in her hand and she had a shocked look on her face, but she was still stunningly beautiful, with her great mess of curly hair and an expression of intense innocence, which Felix thought she had no God-given right to possess.

"Soraya, baby," Edwige said.

"Don't fall out and start crying," Soraya said. "I'm in the middle of an argument with this one." She jutted her chin up at Felix.

"He's treating you wrong now? I'll kick his ass," Edwige said.

"That's not what you were saying the other night," Soraya said.

Felix sighed. He checked up and down the hallway. Edwige reached out and put a hand on Felix's chest.

"You're not taking care of her right, you'll answer to me," Edwige said. "And I can make you sing all night long."

Felix's phone rang as he removed Edwige's hand.

"Excuse me," he said.

He stepped out in the hallway to take the call.

Edwige stood with Soraya. Her voice changed and she said, "You all right? I heard about Gus and called your cell, but it's not on."

"Yeah, 'cause I can't have people calling me now," Soraya said. "And no, I'm not all right."

The door opened and Felix stepped in.

"That was Franklin. He's meeting with Vasquez. I've got to get across town. You promise me you'll be okay?"

"The big boy demands a promise," Edwige said, her voice beyond seductive. When nobody said anything, Edwige went on, "You two still have an unconsummated thing for each other? Because if that's not the case, I wouldn't mind taking a ride."

"Cut it out. I'm in mourning."

"I've got to go," Felix said. "Call and I'll be here. If you see trouble, do us all a favor and don't doubt that it's for real."

Felix moved around Edwige and went out. In the doorway he tipped his hat and strode down the hall.

Soraya and Edwige watched him go.

"Felix looks at you like he loves you," Edwige said. She began to stroke Soraya's hair. "And it isn't like a brotherly love, either. Are you dealing with that?" She sat on Soraya's bed and crossed her legs.

"Not right now, baby," Soraya said. "It's way too much for right now." She gave her friend a half smile and let her know that she was just tired. She slipped her hair into a ponytail and stretched. Then she pulled off her black sweater and found a red denim shirt, buttoned it over her bra. She exhaled and looked at Edwige, who was examining the contents of her bag.

"A Vicodin'd help," Edwige said. "Now we need to deal with this. Did you speak to your mom?"

"Yeah," Soraya said. "But I didn't tell her that I'm deep in it." She closed the door. The room was quiet around them and the curtain was drawn, so there wasn't much light. The only smell was Edwige's handmade sandalwood perfume.

"You better call her. She reads the papers. She knew that Gus used?"

Soraya sat down next to Edwige on the bed.

"She knew," Soraya said. She had her head in her hands. "My mother knew all about Gus. And she warned me against him. And I told her she was wrong."

And then Edwige was holding Soraya's head because Soraya was sobbing. It had been a little over thirty hours since she'd gotten the news. She'd held most of it back in front of Felix, and it hadn't even been an effort. But now she couldn't stop.

"It's okay, baby," Edwige said. "Tough girls like us have got to stick together."

"I left her with her friend Edwige," Felix told his father. He'd taken a cab across the park and now he stood with his father in front of the Nineteenth Precinct station house.

"Get back to her within three hours," Franklin said. "It'll take that long or less for whoever has her gun to figure out who she is and where she is."

"I was thinking two," Felix said. They walked up the marble steps together and uniformed cops made way for them. As usual, a lot of the uniforms recognized Franklin. As usual, they were divided. Some snubbed him or muttered "asshole" under their breath. The rest smiled and seemed to want to ask him how they could get to where he was. Franklin appeared to be lost in thought, though, and not a single cop dared to approach him.

They went over to the sergeant at the desk and declared

their business. He waved them over to an interrogation room without saying a word. He didn't have them sign in, didn't have them show ID. Nothing.

"Unofficial visit," Franklin said. "These cops don't want a record that we're here."

"Vasquez wants us invisible, why didn't he meet us at his daughter's diner?" Felix asked.

"He must have something he can't take away from here," Franklin said. "Be nice to Vasquez. He's working with us."

"I'm always nice," Felix said.

"Let's take 'always' one day at a time."

They went into an empty interrogation room and sat down, took the free moment to compose themselves.

Felix rubbed his clean-shaven face. He and his father looked about as good as they ever had. He'd slept through the night. No nightmares. He'd been on the couch with Soraya and he'd slept lightly, but he'd had no horrible dreams, no black holes, no violence. Peace. He knew it was because he had someone to guard. That that's what he was: a watchdog.

Before he could stop himself, he said, "Wasn't I good with Stuart Apple?" And then he bit his tongue.

Franklin was about to respond when Eitel Vasquez came through the door. He was in a pin-striped putty-colored suit and black shirt. No tie. He walked into the room, slammed the door behind him, kicked it twice with his heel, and scratched his chest. He looked at the Novaks as if they were garbage that he'd forgotten to take out and that explained why the room stank.

"I see you brought your son," Vasquez said. "Him, I don't want to hear anything from."

"No problem," Felix said, and smiled.

"Good," Vasquez said. He sat down heavily on a wooden

chair across from the Novaks. He breathed out and shook his head. "It's like this: Now Miguel says he was talking to protect somebody else. That he was doing it all for a friend."

"What friend?" Franklin said.

"I got her outside."

"It's a lady?" Franklin said.

"Like everybody, she has a story. Miguel loves her, apparently."

"I don't get it," Franklin said.

Vasquez rubbed his forehead. "When this is over, we're going to have a talk about how your time was down at Wackenhut. I'd rather move down to Florida and guard rich people for the rest of my life than do four more years in Homicide. People's logic is not just bizarre, it is beyond the scope of my comprehension. And I, for one, am sick of it." Then he yelled, "Bring her in."

The door opened and an extremely short uniformed cop led in a small woman in her forties. She wore jeans and a pair of sneakers, but she had on a silky red shirt with several buttons undone. Her breasts were huge and the outlines of the dense cups of her bra were visible. Her hair was in a long ponytail that snaked down her back.

Vasquez said, "This is Victoria Lampado, Miguel's girlfriend."

"Not anymore," Victoria said. She smiled. Felix recognized her smell. It was the scent of the sheets at the Sutherland. Fabric softener and white lilies.

"I didn't come to you," Victoria said quickly, turning to Vasquez. "To you I would not say a thing because you smell like 116th Street in summer when there is no rain for days."

Vasquez shook his head. "I've heard her act before. Keep her. All of you walk out the door when you're done. You need to hear her story and then we can connect it to whoever hired her ex. I'm on the trail of her man now. Fuckin' Zorro. This'll make sense when she's done."

Vasquez opened the door, walked out, slammed it behind him.

"Who is this?" Victoria asked, nodding at Felix.

"That's my son," Franklin said.

"Very nice. Now let me tell you my story." She smiled, leaned back in her chair, passed a hand over her chest. "For six years I've worked at the Sutherland. All that time I had two lovers. Neither knew the other one. How could I handle two men, each with such burning desire? I did it." She shook her head and smiled. "I did it with ease."

"One was Miguel Santorez," Felix said.

"Yes. That is true. But the other one, he was tall and thin. Not like Miguel. Perhaps a little—effeminate? Yes. He worked with us for some time in the laundry room, but then he was promoted. And I only saw him in the guest rooms, where we made love. Afterward he would leap from the bed!"

Victoria jumped a bit in her chair and Felix moved slightly, too, reflexively. Victoria laughed at Felix, and her great bosom shook.

"He would jump from the bed and take out his stiletto. And he would whip it out and show me his skills! He was wonderful. But . . ." She stopped, and her eyes grew full.

"But," Franklin prompted after she didn't go on.

"But someday I knew he was going to kill with it."

She drooped her head to one side. Felix watched her. He thought she was incredibly sexy, in a way that he knew he was far too young to understand.

"So why did Vasquez go after Miguel if he didn't do anything wrong?"

"My Miguel missed a couple of days of work after some things we did together. Then his wife threw him out. It was nothing. Men go missing from the Sutherland all the time. The work conditions are horrendous. And that dumb *maricón* cop—we gave him the tip-off and he went out and got the wrong man."

"Your Miguel," Franklin said. "So why'd he confess?"

Victoria gave him an incredulous look. She said, "They hit him, of course. And they told him what to say. But when they told him who they thought he was, he realized who the killer must be. And Miguel, my smaller lover, he decided that he'd be better off in jail for life than to have my Angel know that he was with me, too. Because Angel would kill Miguel."

Victoria used her hands as fans and tried to cool herself down.

"This is hard to believe," Franklin said.

"Passion is volatile," Felix said.

"The boy is right! And so when I understood what was happening, I came to this police station and told that pig my story. Now they're looking for my lover, Angel Pooley. And my little Miguel was sprung onto the street. He's hiding in his house like a scared little ferret. You go out and find my Angel Pooley. You find him and you ask him who would make him do such things with his stiletto. And I will go to my Miguel."

She stood up, heaved her great chest, winked at Felix, and walked out.

Franklin and Felix sat in the interrogation room for a moment before speaking. Felix leaned forward, ran his finger over the cigarette burns in the old table. Then he leaned farther forward, smelled the air where Victoria had been sitting. He imagined she'd worked the night shift. Maybe she'd had a few drinks at home before putting on her coat and coming down to the police station.

"Somebody hired an in-house killer," Franklin said.

"Simon," Felix said. "Then when Pooley disappeared,

Simon tried to get Gus to do some more. Gus said no, and Simon shot him."

"It could also be that no one hired her Angel Pooley at all. That he did this thing himself," Franklin said.

"What about the earpiece?"

"Talking to God," Franklin said, but his voice was flat. "I doubt that Victoria Lampado was sleeping with somebody else's hired killer, but who knows? Maybe she's fingering everybody she doesn't like and protecting someone else."

"We should ask her if it is that way."

But when they came out of the interrogation room, Victoria Lampado was gone, and so was Eitel Vasquez. He was out already, on Angel Pooley's trail.

"Let's let him take care of the new suspects and we can watch the people we already know," Franklin said. He got on the phone to Gennardi. When he was done, he turned to his son. "Now I need a couple of hours."

Felix nodded. He knew well enough that there were some things his father was going to do that he wasn't going to share with him.

"We're watching Simon now," Gennardi said to Franklin, who was on the phone. He was with Philip in the van on the corner of Third Avenue and East Fiftieth Street.

"No, he's not up to much. He went into a building at 850. Could be doing anything up there. He's got a black car taking him around, a BMW, same as his cousin. Yeah, we'll let you know."

Gennardi hung up. He turned to Philip and sighed. He had a tired look around his eyes and his skin was pouchy and gray.

"Three little Apples," he said. "I see them dancing in my sleep."

"Men or apples?" Philip asked. "How many days in the hotel now?"

It took Gennardi a few moments to answer. "What is this? Thursday afternoon? Four, I think."

"You don't hire a killer in a nice white building like 850 Third," Philip said. "You go in there for an urgent meeting, you're doing business the white-collar way."

"Who're the tenants?"

"Mostly boutique law firms," Philip said. He had a PDA in his lap and he was on the Web, going through the tenants at 850.

"That guy probably sees his lawyer as often as I go to an ATM machine," Gennardi said.

Philip got a call on his phone and began speaking rapidly in Zimbabwean. He sighed, suddenly and long. Neither man's eyes strayed much from the front of 850. Simon came out and got into his car. He was dressed in a black suit and a sky blue shirt with two buttons left undone. The shirt had a high collar and the pants were tailored tight around his ankles. His thick black hair looked as if it had been sculpted from marble. He didn't look around him on the street. Didn't hesitate as he slipped into his car.

"This guy isn't nervous," Philip said as Gennardi started the van. "I wonder if the only thing he's doing that's illegal is being an arrogant prick."

Simon's driver took him straight to his office, just a few blocks north. Gennardi followed. They had a clear view of Simon in the back of the car. He'd crossed his legs and was reading a copy of the *Spectator,* the page-eight gossip column. Gennardi parked halfway up the street.

"I wonder what the other cousin is up to," Philip said. He drummed lightly on the door panel.

"We're supposed to watch this one," Gennardi said. He

had a rosary in his hands and he was threading it through his fingers. It made a sound like stiff joints loosening after a long night of sleep.

"This businessman is boring me; let's watch the one with the victim complex," Philip said.

"Okay," Gennardi said. "Executive decision. We're switching surveillance targets. We'll find the sad sack, see what he's up to." Gennardi keyed the ignition and they swung west and headed toward Park Avenue.

19

Franklin and Felix sat in the lounge at LaGuardia's United terminal. It was just before dawn on Friday morning, and they watched through massive windows as the ground crew drove around in their carts, loading up the early morning commuter planes.

They sipped coffee and paged through the morning newspapers. The *Spectator* had a page-two article about the hotel murders, which basically said that there were no suspects but that occupancy rates in Apple properties had dropped 70 percent in two days. There was a puff piece on Eitel Vasquez that Lanie had written, but it provided almost no information save that Vasquez was popular in his community and was looking forward to retiring in Florida. The *Post* was taking another tack with the story—they had a piece on how to protect yourself in an elevator, with a diagram that showed the potential power of a body slam.

"A little late," Franklin said as he showed the piece to Felix. "Maybe if you treated her a little nicer, she'd give us some help."

"She doesn't know anything," Felix said. "Starling's alone, right? Maybe he'd like to take her out."

"That's sick," Franklin said. "Starling is literally three times her age. Don't talk like that in front of me."

"Sorry," Felix said, and tipped his hat over his eyes.

Franklin went through the other papers. They hadn't dropped the story, but they'd also taken it off the front pages. It had only been nine days, but the connections between the killings were frayed. And Stuart Apple had hired Alfred Rubinstein's PR firm to spin the story, so now it appeared that he was the victim of a few small, isolated, and deeply unfortunate incidents.

Felix said, "Says here Stuart Apple is cooperating with police. That he believes the initial murder was done by some-one inside his hotel. A labor dispute issue gone ballistic."

"Could be," Franklin said. "Though as you'll recall, he didn't say that to us. He's just making suggestions, muffling the impact of what he thinks is the truth."

"Which is?"

"The junk about his nephew. Either he put that stuff together himself or his son fed it to him. A distinction, by the way, that we need to worry about."

Felix turned to his father. "Tell me, why can't we just call these Texans on the phone? Why do we have to fly up there to see them?"

Franklin didn't speak for a moment. A JetBlue plane took off, and they watched the brightly colored plane streak into the clouds. No sound made it through the windows, though jet fuel seemed to hang heavy in the air. The sun was rising over Riker's Island, and Franklin looked out at it. He turned and smiled at his son.

He said, "These men are in mourning. They want to move through their sadness and we're going to help them. That's our job. That's why we're going up there. You take on a client and it's immediately personal. Don't let anybody tell you otherwise."

"I see."

They got up and boarded the plane, which was nearly empty save for a few Dartmouth professors and some sales-men. Franklin and Felix spread out over several seats.

"Where'd you sleep last night if you weren't at the Sutherland and you're no longer with Lanie?"

"I checked in at Soraya's dorm room at about four. But before that I was in your office," Felix said. "I vacuumed, actually. And I did some filing. I took apart your shotguns and cleaned them out. The Mossberg was really crying out for it. Then I wrote out a timeline for the case. And I crossed that with who was where, when as far as we know. There's fewer blank spots than you'd think."

"So you didn't sleep."

"No."

"How is Soraya?"

"Not good," Felix said. "But she's got Edwige with her all the time now, which helps."

When they arrived in New Hampshire, the same driver was waiting for them.

"How's the Magnum working out?" the driver asked as they drove into the compound.

"Real good," Franklin said. "You swing that thing around in Manhattan, you can stop traffic on Broadway at rush hour."

"I'll bet. A well-aimed round would knock a city bus right off its route."

"The truth is, I haven't had a chance to fire it yet," Franklin said.

"Well, man! You gotta fire it!" the driver said, and then he wouldn't say another thing.

"He's just like Richard the waiter," Franklin said to Felix. "He takes my foibles personal."

This time the Texas husbands were in the lodge. It was nearly lunchtime and they were standing in front of a fire-place that was nearly as tall as they were. They greeted the Novaks quietly, and when each man had been given coffee, they asked for the details of the case.

"There's a thing we didn't tell you," Ed Wallingford said after Franklin had outlined what they knew so far. Franklin watched Ed's face, which revealed no flicker of anything that resembled resentment.

"First we'd like some time with the button man. Then we'll need access to the Apple who put him up to it."

"We're not ready to say which Apple yet. Or how many," Franklin said.

"Sure, you are," Ed said. "You just don't want to say."

"Maybe that's so," Franklin said.

"We're going home Sunday from New York. We'll be in town Saturday night, staying at the Algonquin. We figure this thing ought to be wrapped up by then. Wouldn't you say?"

"Yes," Franklin said. "I would, actually."

"That's our man," Ed said. He clapped Franklin on the back. "We're not asking you to take these men down. We just want names and locations, that's all. You got our check."

"I did," Franklin said. Felix thought his father's face was as stiff as Tom Stowe's.

"Let's go out back and shoot," Tom Stowe said. The four men walked out of the lodge. A young man came up and handed Tom a Weatherby Athena.

"Handsome gun," Franklin said. "Walnut stocks, plenty of brass and engraving. That's a fine piece of equipment."

Tom walked fifteen yards down a hill toward a cleared area that looked down on an ice blue lake. Some geese flew overhead. Tom dropped to one knee and aimed at the sky. The noise from his shot echoed against the lodge. He shot again and a goose left the flock, headed in a straight vertical line down toward the water. It hit hard and some of its feathers were carried away in the ripples made by the impact.

"Good shot," Ed said. But his voice was weary.

Tom stood up. He was shaking slightly. He stood alone on the top of the hill for a moment before he rejoined the three men. His lower lip was trembling. He held his shotgun loosely, in the crook of his right arm. His shirt was open at the neck and he wore no hat, but he didn't appear to be cold.

"We haven't heard much from you, Tom," Franklin said.

Tom turned around. He said, "We know that someone connected to you was killed since you've taken on our case. We're sorry for that."

"We're not sure that murder was related," Franklin said. His voice was dry.

"They'll come after someone you love next. You know how these things are done."

"Yes," Franklin said. "We know that. We're protecting her."

"Cowards lash out with little thought for consequence," Tom said. "It's true all over the world. In the end it'll be us or them."

"We'll see you in New York tomorrow or the next night," Franklin said. He turned to go. Tom reached out then and grabbed Felix by the arm. He said, "Your father's a good man. Find out who did this. Find out before they murder someone you love."

Franklin watched as Felix stood still, gave the client in mourning his full attention. The only sound that could be heard was the cry of geese above them.

"We'll find out," Felix said. "You won't go back to Texas without an answer."

The Novaks stood in the Manchester airport at the Cheers bar, eating roast beef sandwiches and drinking Budweiser. A television above the bar was tuned to CNN, and they watched steadily as reporters recounted good and bad news about the economy. It was only three in the afternoon, but the bar was dark.

"Tom Stowe was wrong when he said that cowards lash out without thought of consequence," Franklin said. "Maybe that's true in Texas, but not in New York. Cowards are just like anybody else. They come in all shapes and sizes. They act all different ways. Live by an aphorism like that, you die by it."

"Maybe that's why Tom generally keeps his mouth shut," Felix said.

"No, that probably isn't why. I think it's hard for him to speak without crying," Franklin said. "He loved his wife."

"He's a good man."

"I don't know if I agree with that. The time they want with the button man and the access to the Apples?" Franklin asked. "They want to kill the people who did this. It'll be hard to stop them."

They listened in silence as an announcement came over the PA system. Their plane was delayed.

20 It was nearly dusk on Friday when Gennardi and Philip drove by Morris Apple's town house. This was the third time they'd passed it.

"How'd we start suspecting the Apples in the first place?" Philip asked.

Gennardi chewed on that for a moment before answering. Then he said, "I haven't been in on the Apple meetings. But every time a Novak or Soraya talks to one of them, they finger-point. And nobody asked them to. That's been the basis so far. That and our presumption of greed on their parts. Of nasty, all-encompassing greed."

Neither man spoke for a few minutes. Save some hours where they'd gone to their hotel rooms to sleep, they'd been in the van for nearly two days. Nothing had happened. They made every effort to keep the van clean. But it was hopeless. Philip's lunch from an Eritrean restaurant on Third Avenue and Gennardi's Caesar salad that he'd gotten in a takeaway carton from Elaine's had stunk up the cab. There were newspapers in bunches behind them. They'd tried to fold them neatly, but they'd shifted in transit. Then there were the paper coffee cups, the supplies they used to clean their guns, extra pairs of shoes, the Newcon optic BN-5 binoculars, tactical laser attachments, and all the other surveillance gear. It was a mess. And there was nothing they could do about it but wish for action.

"Maybe they just suspect each other because that's all they know how to do. Like military generals or members of a royal family."

"Or anybody who's rich," Gennardi said. They rounded the corner onto East Sixty-third Street again. There was nothing on it but dog walkers and black cars waiting to make their pickups.

"So maybe it's bullshit, this connection."

"Maybe," Gennardi said. "Meanwhile some fucking Zorro is running around with his head spinning, looking for the next out of towner to off. And we're watching a fat kid with a trust fund who sleeps in his mommy's bed."

"Yeah," Philip said. "And if I'm anything but piss bored, it's only my mother who knows it. Why don't you give Eitel Vasquez a call, see what his story is with Angel Pooley or see if the Novaks are back from the woods?"

Gennardi nodded. He pulled his cell phone from the breast pocket of his blazer.

"After this pass I will," he said.

They slowed as they passed Morris's house. They watched his door to the street, which was small, with a white buzzer embedded in the stone on its left. Just then Morris came out. He wore a brown trench coat with the collar up and black boots. He began to walk rapidly toward Fifth Avenue. It was easy to follow him. There was just enough traffic. He hailed a cab on Fifth.

"Son of a mongrel bitch," Philip said. "Doesn't he have a driver?"

Gennardi nodded. He put his phone away. The cab disappeared in the drive across the park and they moved along after it.

"The West Side?" Philip said. "I wonder why."

The cab turned right on Central Park West and headed north.

"Uh-oh," Gennardi said. "He's going to visit his new friend."

"Soraya," Philip said.

Gennardi was already dialing her number.

"It's no big deal yet," Gennardi said. "But it could be."

Soraya and Edwige were wasting the day together in Edwige's dorm room. They were drinking good red wine, a

Rioja that Edwige's father had sent her from a commercial he was shooting in Brazil. They had candles going and they'd been alternating Mary J. Blige and Badly Drawn Boy. Soraya didn't like BDB, but Edwige was friends with him, so she tolerated it.

She was lying on Edwige's bed, bundled in a silvery cashmere blanket that was incredibly warm and weighed nothing at all. She waved her hands through the smoky air. Edwige was in her white bubble chair. She had her eyes closed and she was stroking Irpa, the little cat that she kept in her dorm room, which was in violation of half a dozen Barnard regulations. But of course Edwige didn't give a shit. Her father's accountant paid the fines.

"Hungry?" Edwige asked.

"Not yet," Soraya said.

"Cool, me neither," Edwige said.

They'd planned on ordering Chinese food from Mr. Chow. They were going to blow off the whole night, too. At the end of the bed Soraya's cell phone rang and she pushed it with her big toe, watched it ring.

"Couldn't be good news," Edwige said.

"No," Soraya said, and sighed. She picked up her phone, said, "Hello?"

"I need to see you," Morris Apple said. "I'm so scared."

"I'm with Edwige," Soraya said.

Soraya listened to the quiet on the other end of the line. There was honking, and she wondered if Morris was already on his way.

"Please, I need to see you alone," Morris said.

Soraya's other line beeped. Gennardi.

"Hold on," Soraya said to Morris.

"Soraya? Morris Apple's headed toward Barnard. He's about a block away."

"I've got him on the other line," Soraya said. "What's going on? Where are you guys?"

"We're following him."

"I thought you were watching Simon."

"No—he's all about business. At least we think he is. Listen to me, this is bad news either way. If there are people watching him who aren't us, then he's leading them straight to you. If he's the one who's doing . . ." Gennardi trailed off.

"Where are Franklin and Felix?" Soraya asked.

"Stuck on a plane," Gennardi said. "Look, you should see him. We don't want to scare him, no matter what he is. Take him to a bar, do whatever you need to do, but keep him out in the open and we'll watch, okay?"

"Done," Soraya said. "We'll be coming out the entrance on 113th Street. We'll go to the West End. Actually, you guys go there."

Soraya stood up. She clicked over to the other line, said, "Where are you?"

"I'm on the West Side. I'm in a cab," Simon said.

"We can meet for a drink. Go to the West End Bar on Broadway. Wait for me there. I might bring Edwige—"

"No," Morris said.

"Ease off," Soraya said. "I bring who I want. You ask something from me, you don't tell me how it's going to be." She ended the call.

"Fucking dominatrix," Edwige said.

Soraya nodded. "Let's go listen to this rich boy."

While Edwige was getting dressed, Soraya called Gennardi and confirmed the plan.

In the Roadrunner, headed back from LaGuardia, Franklin and Felix didn't speak. They sped along Astoria Boulevard. Felix stroked his clean chin, one finger on the bottom of the steering wheel. He tried to imagine how he'd behave if he were afraid of someone close to him.

Franklin's phone rang. Felix watched his father's face as he took the call. He watched his eyes as he turned over the case, looked at the angles, the implications, the bits of meaning that revealed themselves too slowly. And Felix saw that as he thought analytically, as the anger in him drained away, he'd become a better detective, smarter, more professional.

"What was it?" Felix asked.

"Vasquez took down our thin man at the Sutherland. He says we should stop by, mention Victoria Lampado, see what the reveal is."

"What was this thin man doing?"

"Watching the guests. Jiggling a stiletto in his pocket."

"His name is Angel Pooley?" Felix asked.

"Yeah. He's white. Black trench coat, the whole bit."

Felix whistled, low. He felt relieved that now Soraya must be safer since the real murderer was no longer on the streets. He was sure she couldn't be in as much danger now. He said, "Then what the hell was he doing at the Sutherland?"

"Nobody said the killer was smart. But you're missing something." Franklin turned to his son and smiled. "This shithead takes directions, right? Maybe somebody decided it was time he got caught."

Felix nodded. His relief about Soraya disappeared as quickly as it had come. He felt like someone who thinks they see a familiar face and smiles. But they look again, and the face is a stranger's and they're not smiling back. Like fortune, casting its eyes elsewhere.

Felix said, "Dad, let's split up. You take Angel Pooley. I've got to see Soraya."

It'd taken seven months, but this time Felix didn't feel shame or pain when he said Dad. Now he only felt lucky he knew someone who would answer when he called out that name.

Franklin said, "Drop me off uptown. And speed it up, can't you? I thought this thing had an engine."

"Oh, it's got an engine," Felix said. He hit the gas harder and the Roadrunner took off.

Philip and Gennardi sat at the bar at the West End and waited for Soraya to arrive. It was Friday night, happy hour. Felix had just called Philip, and under the bar Philip had text-messaged their location and what was going on. Felix could come in, he could walk right by where Soraya would be sitting with Edwige and Morris. He could sit in the next booth and order a hamburger and complain that it was overdone. Because as far as anyone knew, Morris didn't know what Felix looked like or even who he was. If he did show recognition, that would work against him. So that was how they planned to play it.

Over the last few years the West End had morphed from a college spot to a neighborhood place and there was dancing where the bulk of the restaurant had been. So now, while Gennardi and Philip sipped Guinness, the sounds of the Pointer Sisters singing "I'm So Excited" surrounded them, and twenty or thirty souls who were only happy that it was almost the weekend threw their hands in the air and screamed.

Soraya came in with Edwige. They walked toward an empty booth at the back, near the stairs that went down to the bathrooms. Within seconds Morris followed them in. They sat down together, and Morris stared at Edwige.

He said, "Now I don't feel like I can say anything because she's here."

"Sorry," Soraya said.

A waiter came over, a tall man with a patient face.

"What can I get you ladies?" he asked.

"I'll have sparkling water," Morris said. "Please bring me the sealed bottle—Pellegrino if you've got it."

"We're drinking cheap red wine," Edwige said. "Whatever you're pouring is fine. Just splash it around in a couple of beer mugs."

The waiter shrugged and went back to the bar. Morris looked after him. He pulled his trench coat over his round shoulders and shivered.

"Who is that?" Morris said. He was trembling. "That man. I think that's the one who's trying to kill me."

Soraya turned around slowly. She knew that Philip and Gennardi were sitting at the bar. She followed Morris's gaze to a man who sat alone about ten feet down from them. The bartender brought the young man a Budweiser, and the man took it and went and sat in a booth. He watched the NCAA scores on a television that hung above the bar. He was Felix Novak. Soraya thought, Well, that takes care of that.

"Are you out of your mind?" Edwige asked. "That's Felix Novak. Felix!" Edwige called out.

"No," Soraya said. She realized that she hadn't told Edwige that Morris wouldn't know who Felix was. Soraya shook her head and sighed.

Philip and Gennardi stirred. They had the entire square of bar between them and Soraya's booth, but Soraya knew that if they needed to, they'd come across, fast, and take Morris down. She stood up and shook her head vigorously, made a hand signal to convey *stay back.* Philip and Gennardi nodded. But their faces were alert. The rest of the bar was too busy with the excitement of hearing "It's Raining Men" to pay any attention. It was the bar's traditional Sadie Hawkins song. All around them heavyset women with bright eyes and uneven breathing selected semiwilling men and dragged them off to the dance floor.

"I don't understand," Morris said. He was clutching his neck as if he were preparing to protect himself from strangulation.

"No, you sure don't," Edwige said. Her phone rang and she took the call. Felix came over and stood at the table. He had his beer in his hand and he seemed entirely calm, though his other hand was hidden slightly behind his back and tucked into his waistband.

Felix said, "Hi, Edwige. Hi, Soraya."

Morris said, "I saw him meeting with my uncle and cousin. It was him and one of the ugliest bald men I've ever seen. I'm sure he's one of the killers they hired. Can't you call the police or someone and have him taken away?"

Felix nodded once as he listened. He said, "You really think that was the ugliest bald man you ever laid eyes on?"

"By far," Morris said. He was crouching down in the booth, readying himself for a blow.

"Damn," Felix said. "I wonder if that'd hurt his feelings."

He turned to Philip and Gennardi and swept a hand across his chest. Dead operation. But instead of walking over to them, he just walked out into the street.

"Simon never mentioned to you that anybody was investigating the murder of those Texas sisters?" Soraya asked.

Morris shook his head. He said, "I don't understand why you'd know that man."

"It's an awfully long story," Soraya said. "I don't have time to tell it now. Tell me, have you ever seen anyone—I'm not saying you don't have a right to be paranoid—but have you ever discussed your fears with a professional? Like a therapist?"

"Are you kidding?" Morris asked. "Why do you think I

came across town? I thought you'd make me feel better, and I need you. But for everyday problems I see a behaviorist and a psychoanalyst, twice a week for each. I'm on Klonopin, Vicodin, and I take OxyContin, too. Though it's been more difficult to find lately."

"I'm on Klonopin," Edwige said. "How do you like it?"

"I love it. But sometimes I wonder if it doesn't make me a little jumpy," Morris said. "I think that's why I wanted to see you, because I thought you'd calm me down."

"I thought it was supposed to calm you down," Soraya said.

"I did, too," Morris said. "My behaviorist and my psychoanalyst are having lunch next weekend in London to talk about what to try next. I'm sending them there to talk to Catherine Crockatt at the Corrigan Clinic. She's been on my case for years. But sometimes I feel like none of them know even half of what I'm really up to. I think I need to go home now."

And he did.

21 Franklin walked into the Nineteenth Precinct alone. Vasquez had left instructions with the desk that he was to be escorted to the same interrogation room where he and Felix had spoken to Victoria Lampado. The same desk sergeant waved him along. The same air of mean-spirited indolence pervaded the place. The only difference was that now there were two uniforms outside the interrogation room and Franklin had to sign a form.

"Where are the TV cameras?" Franklin asked the older of the two uniforms.

"Commissioner'll be here in half an hour. They'll make it here on his heels."

"There's another way out?" Franklin asked.

The older guy pointed down the corridor to a dimly lit red Exit sign. He was a sullen-looking type with skin the color of rolling paper.

"Go through the door on the right. That takes you down to our basement. You make a right at the third door down there, follow that through to the four doors that are painted brown. Take the one on your far left. Come up a staircase. That lets you out through a Chinese takeout around the corner. Mee Noodle Shop. I recommend the chicken wings and french fries."

"Thanks," Franklin said.

"Anytime you need somebody for enforcement work, you call me," the uniform said. He tapped his plastic nameplate, which said Udo in capital letters.

"I'll remember," Franklin said.

Inside the green-painted room Eitel Vasquez sat with a young man with thinning hair who was smoking a cigarette and staring fixedly at a point above the door to the room.

Vasquez was also quiet. He had a *Spectator* in front of him and he was rustling the pages.

"Hello there," Franklin said. His voice was soft. "You like the piece on you? Apparently you're the best homicide guy in the NYPD."

"Don't yank my cock," Vasquez said. "I know you placed the piece. You think I don't know who your father-in-law is? I'm not saying I don't appreciate it, but I got a better question. You believe this twee little jammy couldn't get a better piece of ass than Victoria Lampado?" Vasquez asked. Then he laughed. He actually slapped his thigh. Franklin watched the young man. He continued to smoke.

"She's got gifts that you and I might not know how to appreciate," Franklin said.

"Bullshit," Vasquez said. "She's a spent piece of laundry room trash that only a queen'd screw." Vasquez glared at Franklin and then winked. Good cop, bad cop.

Franklin shrugged. He said, "Vasquez, you wouldn't know a lady who fucks with class if she knocked you down in the street and shoved a hand down your pants."

"Who's this, anyway?" Angel Pooley asked. He jutted his chin at Franklin. His left hand was handcuffed to the chair, so he only gestured with his shoulder.

"Private operative. Old enemy of mine. Guy's not after you. He's interested in the money trail."

"I can't figure why you'd run around killing old ladies just for shits and giggles," Franklin said. He sat down suddenly and came face-to-face with Pooley. "So I came to ask you about it."

"Hey, who the fuck cares what you came to do. I just asked who you were," Angel Pooley said.

"I'm sorry. May I call you Angel?" Franklin asked. The man nodded. He had black eyes and very long eyelashes.

There were freckles on his forehead and his neck. Effeminate, Franklin thought. The stiletto fit.

"He give up the setup, the earpiece and all that shit?" Franklin asked Vasquez.

"Not a bit of it," Vasquez said. "Till I hear different, here's what I'm thinking. The earpiece? Connected to the air. The joke about getting instructions from God? Turns out it was true. This fucker's a medium-range psycho. We play it cool, make sure the bruises don't show, the DA'll put him in a chair unless he froths from the mouth during trial or some such—not that I'm making the suggestion."

Franklin said, "You said the same thing about Miguel Santorez and now he's hiding under his bed with some Hershey bars and a copy of *Juggs* magazine, waiting for Victoria Lampado to come home."

Then nobody spoke for a minute. There was waiting. Franklin sat back. He smiled at Angel Pooley.

"I'm not like that fucking Miguel," Angel Pooley said. "I'm not copping or talking or giving up any of my shit. You see me, you know I'm hard. I got friends in all the max facilities and the supermaxes and all the rest. So I don't give a fuck what you faggots throw down. I'll do my eight to ten or whatever, and . . ." Angel Pooley stopped speaking.

Franklin said, "You seem to have grown pensive."

"Fuck you, old man. You're not even a cop."

"I'm interested in the Apples," Franklin said. "Not you."

"Apples? I don't know shit about that, either."

"You don't know shit," Franklin said, "about a lot of things."

"I know you got a case you can't solve. You got somebody who was killed with a bullet, somebody else who fell down an elevator shaft, and you caught me and I only carry a knife."

"The women in the elevator," Franklin said. "The man in the

penthouse. The threat of additional killings at the Sutherland. These things point to an unhappy ex-employee. Your lover came in here, she told a story. The story was about you."

Angel Pooley shook his head. He smiled and his teeth were clean and white. He was surprisingly symmetrical for a killer, Franklin thought. He was used to guys who did killings in part because they were ugly and it pissed them off. He thought that Angel Pooley had been given gifts and he'd used them poorly.

Angel Pooley said, "You got questions for Apples, talk to Apples. I'm done. I know I'm headed upstate. I already got my boys making my bed at Sing Sing."

Vasquez said, "We told him about the voice recognition we got from the elevator video. We're running DNA tests now and all the rest of the coroner shit. He's right to think that a confession'll ease his passage."

"Which Apple should I talk to?" Franklin asked.

"The young smart one," Angel Pooley whispered. "Now you owe me."

Then Angel Pooley shook his head, and Franklin understood that there was no way he'd answer the next question, which was, Which Apple is smart? Franklin stood up.

"You going to keep him here?" Franklin asked Vasquez.

"No room. He'll go to Riker's on a bus tonight."

"It's always the bitches who give you up," Angel said. He laughed.

Franklin wandered into the corridor and called Felix, told him what he'd learned.

Felix said, "I'm going to give my young friend Simon Apple a call. Nobody ever called him stupid."

"I have information," Felix said. He'd called Joanne Gordimer and she'd patched him through to Simon's cell phone. Felix had a Sacagawea dollar in his hand and he threaded it through his fingers slowly, then faster, till it looked like it was moving of its own accord.

"Well, we should go ahead and meet," Simon said. "At the Sperling. I'm thinking of redoing the lobby there when I'm done with the Sutherland."

"Upgrading the whole line," Felix said.

"That's right. Meet me in the lobby in an hour."

Felix took the extra time to drive down Fifth Avenue in the Roadrunner. It was Friday, rush hour. But Fifth was cool. He looked up at the trees and thought about the idea of vacation. He'd never taken one. Farm life didn't allow it, and since he'd been in New York, he didn't think about things like leisure. Now he wondered if he might take Soraya somewhere. They could sit on a beach, drink brightly colored cocktails, like at the end of heist movies. The traffic inched along. He breathed deep and closed his eyes for a moment, relaxing.

The Sperling lobby was nothing special. The requisite check-in counter was a dark wood that could have been anything—oak, cherry, painted ply. The carpets were brown and the walls were an inexplicable bluish white. Felix thought that the place looked like the Sutherland's cheap relation from the sticks.

The lobby was deserted when he arrived, save for an attractive young woman in a black blazer and white shirt who stood behind the check-in counter and made a point of not seeing him. She looked down and Felix could tell from her hand movements that she was playing a game on her handheld.

Felix sank down in a green leather chair in the forty-foot-square waiting area. He was surrounded by other, similar green chairs and couches. He put his foot up on a black steel table in front of him and pulled his jacket closed against the flat fall air that gusted in when some German backpackers entered the lobby. He felt just young enough to enjoy being weary, but he didn't indulge the feeling. If Simon was their man, he thought he was fooling everyone. He'd set up his cousin and caused enough turmoil in his father's business to point to his own need to eventually run the company. He hadn't even said he suspected his cousin. He'd tricked his father into doing that.

It'd be difficult to figure out how to arrest him, if it came to that, Felix thought. He'd have a stunning legal team and he'd know that when it was all over, he could still run his operation. But he might crack. He might kill his cousin on the way down. He might kill his father. Felix shivered and sighed.

"Is that lounge chair at all comfortable?" Simon asked. He stood above Felix and looked down at him. He wore blue jeans and a pair of slip-on moccasins. His blue blazer was cashmere and his yellow shirt had the thick high collar that Europeans favored. Even Felix had to hand it to him—he looked terrific.

"It isn't bad," Felix said. "But I've been sitting in your chairs for days. They all feel good to me."

Felix felt his .45 nestled against his ribs. At this range he'd bang the butt of the gun against Simon's head before Simon could shoot him. He hadn't shot anyone yet, but he did know how to level the gun, how to hold it with both hands, place the feet, reduce recoil to almost nothing.

Simon looked quickly around the lobby. More tourists were crowded around the reception area. They looked exhausted, as if they'd just come off an impossibly long flight.

"It's too bad about what happened here, so few days ago," Simon said. "Let's go and have a drink at the Blue

Shade lounge in the back—there's a name I'll be changing. It's nearly six, isn't it?"

Simon turned around and began walking before Felix could answer. Felix got up and followed him. He unbuttoned his jacket and let his hands swing at his sides.

At the back of the hotel Simon rapped on a smoked-glass door and then opened it. This room had half a dozen people in it. They'd come in through an entrance on East Thirty-second Street that Felix hadn't seen earlier. The room had more lounge chairs, but these were black leather. Felix understood that unless his body had been brought from elsewhere, Gus had probably been in this room before he'd died. Of course Eitel Vasquez had been loath to share what information he had—he expected the Novaks to pull a killer and a motive out of a hat like magicians. Felix shook his head. But then he caught Simon's eye and smiled. *Exceed* expectations, he thought. Deliver a criminal and a confession.

"Let's take a table," Simon said. Felix nodded. A red Exit sign glowed at the far end of the room. A fight, perhaps, an argument, and then Gus would go back through that way to the garbage area in the back. The single bullet might have come at any time. They didn't have an ME's report yet, and they would have to wrangle access when it did come.

"That killing won't hurt this place's business," Simon said, as if he'd been listening to Felix think, watching him map out the place. Felix nodded, acknowledging Simon's intuition.

"It's not an important bar," Simon said. "Mostly it fills up with foreign students at night and the tourists on package plans who stay here. But I'm going to change all that."

Simon smiled. His skin, Felix saw, was flawless. Healthy, nearly glowing.

"The new king of the hotel bars," Felix said. "Next you'll

be marrying an overexposed model and trying to produce an independent film."

"I'm already involved in both those arenas. You underestimate me. Tell me what's going on with the case," Simon said. "Is there still a threat of more murders?"

"You hope not," Felix said.

"Of course," Simon said. He smiled. "You think a rash of stabbings is good for business? It isn't."

"I wouldn't know what's good and what isn't for business. I'm not from here."

Simon didn't yawn when Felix tried this tack, but he didn't show a flicker of real interest, either.

"The police arrested a man today. They seem to have gotten the right one this time. He'll admit to the murders in a few days."

"Your clients will be pleased."

"Yes. But there's the issue of what was said on that tape," Felix said. "That bothers them kind of a lot."

"That it appeared as if he was hired." Simon nodded. "And you don't know who hired him? I'm confused. Weren't you at the meeting my father and your . . . father had yesterday? A name was named at that meeting, I believe."

"I'm trying to remember, about that meeting," Felix said so he could buy time. He watched Simon's eyes sparkle. He knew he couldn't tell if a man was lying. No one can. But everyone can see a flicker in someone else's eyes. Some play. Simon tousled his thick hair. He seemed to be enjoying some kind of inward laugh. As if he'd been setting up his cousin for years. Eating the cake and putting the chocolate-smeared knife in his cousin's hands, then running off to his room. Felix felt like he understood. Growing up, before she'd run away, his sister had often done that sort of thing to him.

"Yes, I was there," Felix said. "I see your point."

"And you haven't brought him in yet?"

"Your cousin? That's who we're talking about, isn't it? Your blood."

"Blood?" Simon raised an eyebrow and suddenly looked about him. The bartender was busy pouring beer for the students at the bar, but Simon suddenly raised his voice. "Give us two scotches," he said. "Sound good?" he asked.

"Let me get them for you," Felix said. He stood up. He knew that Simon would allow, even encourage someone to wait on him. The bartender was a harried-looking young woman in a leopard print shirt and too much eye makeup. She was changing the music, moving from old Blondie to old Madonna. The place really did need a top-to-bottom renovation.

"Two Macallans," Felix said. He gestured behind. "He'll pick up the tab."

The tourists seemed to realize that they were being skipped and that there wasn't a thing they could do about it. Felix waited at the bar. The bartender came over with the drinks. She had thick, pouty lips and she looked straight at Felix.

"Did you work here last Tuesday?" Felix asked.

She nodded. She seemed to wait, to encourage him.

"Can we talk when I'm done with him?" Felix asked. He knew that his voice was softer, more confident than it had been in the past.

"Sure," she said. She was looking beyond Felix, at Simon.

"Don't be afraid of him," Felix said.

"Easy for you to say," she said. And Felix left her.

Felix sat down. He smiled and said, "I was going to suggest you get a lawyer in any case, you know, but it occurs to me—"

"I already have a lawyer. A team of them, in fact," Simon said.

"Right, that's what I thought," Felix said. He sipped his drink. He thought, It's you or your father, but most likely it's both of you.

Simon's phone went off and he pulled it out of the breast pocket of his blazer and examined it. He nodded to himself.

"We're here so that I may further impress upon you that the problem is with my cousin. I only have a few more minutes. Is there any specific question I can answer?"

"No. There's a man in custody. The police bumbled around. You can count on them to do that, sure. But eventually people bring them the right man. They count on that. So they've got a killer. He'll talk. My father tells me you can't control a man once he's behind bars. People do funny things once they're inside. They'll make up stories, but if you listen to them long enough, you can figure out the truth."

Simon stood up. He said, "That was edifying. It will be a shame when their suspect gives up my cousin. I hope that you have operatives watching Morris so he doesn't flee. I appreciate you letting me know all these facts. I'll act accordingly."

Felix said, "Morris is a hothouse flower with two dead parents and a Barneys credit card who couldn't scramble eggs with a gun to his head. You and your father aren't like that. You two are very good at what you do."

"We aren't suspects," Simon said. "You forget that."

Simon bent down and took up his glass from the table. He sipped the whiskey and then suddenly, finishing what was left, he tossed the empty glass into the seat that he'd vacated.

"This fucking furniture," he said. "It's such shit. Soon I'll run this entire operation. I'll be so powerful, you'll be telling stories about the drink we just had to your ex-pat country buddies at Hogs and Heifers over on West Street during happy hour. Now, of course, you'll excuse me." Simon buttoned his blazer and looked around briefly.

"I'll just stay here. And think over what you've said," Felix said.

Simon leaned down suddenly so that his face was only six inches from Felix's. "I'm like my father in many ways. I've learned just about all my lessons from him." Simon's breath didn't smell of the whiskey he'd just drunk. He said, "Though I'm a lot better looking than my father, which hasn't hurt. You're just like your father, too. You know that, don't you? We have an awful lot in common. See you around."

He went out of the bar through the back entrance. Felix checked his watch—7 P.M. He didn't move. The bartender turned the stereo up. She looked at Felix and switched the music again, to Nick Cave's "Babe, I'm on Fire."

Felix got up and went to the end of the bar to wait for her. A few more backpackers came in and set their Nalgene water bottles and subway maps down on the bar. The bartender got them glasses of pale-colored beer before she came over to Felix.

"Nice music," Felix said.

"That was Simon Apple."

"He's not a friend," Felix said. "Look, I don't have much time. Have the police talked to you?"

"If they have, then you don't want to? Who are you?"

Felix took a deep breath. "Sorry. I'm Felix Novak. I'm a detective and I'm investigating those murders that happened up at the Sutherland."

"Then why are you asking questions down here?" The bartender looked around her.

"I'm also interested in Gus Moravia and what happened Tuesday night. You knew him?" Felix asked. His mouth felt dry.

"Sure. I ID'd the body for the cops. Everybody knew Gus. But his killing had nothing to do with those two sisters from Texas."

"Why not?"

"He was shot in the belly. That's gangland style."

"Who would want to do that?"

"About a thousand people," the bartender said. Her lips made a perfect horizontal line. "When you work around the hotels and the bars, where everybody's got to hop up on some silly drug before going to work, you can offend somebody pretty damn easily."

"So if you wanted to take him out, you'd do it that way. Wouldn't you? Then you'd throw the gun in the East River, forget the whole thing."

"That's right. The Apples are trying to heat these places up. The high-level dealers are in here every night, jostling for position."

"That's all there was to his death?"

"I'd say so," the bartender said.

"You look like a smart person," Felix said. "But on this score, you're way off."

22 "Let's hole up for the night. Nobody needs us," Felix said. "And tomorrow will be Saturday and maybe we can sleep in."

He was with Soraya in her dorm room. It was a bit like a cabin in a sailboat—about eight feet wide and a dozen feet long, with one big window, a bed, a desk, and a chair. There was nothing else save Soraya's piles of books, her copies of all of the works of Walter Benjamin and Louis Althusser, her *There Are No Children Here* and her *Random Family*. Soraya couldn't afford to fill the room with comfortable furniture the way her friend Edwige did. All she had were the books she refused to sell back at the end of the semester and a closet full of good clothes. So Felix leaned back in the chair with his foot up on the windowsill and looked at Soraya, who was curled up on her bed, wrapped in a green wool army blanket that had belonged to her father twenty years ago.

"Morris called me again," Soraya said.

"What'd he want?"

"To talk about how his family is trying to kill him. He's saying he's going to the newspapers next."

"What'd you tell him?"

"I said I knew a reporter who would kill to talk to him."

"You sent him to Lanie?"

"Yeah," Soraya said.

"He's a freak, but it's Simon we want. Gennardi and Philip are watching him. He's going to get desperate and pop. But I hope Lanie knows what she's doing if she meets him. I can't believe she hasn't called me."

"Things are over with her?"

"They have been for what feels like a long time," Felix said. Gently he came forward in the chair till the front legs touched the floor and he was only a few feet from Soraya.

"If nobody needs us tonight, why is your phone on the table next to your gun?" Soraya asked.

Felix glanced at the table behind him. His .45 was there, next to his cell phone. The keys to the Roadrunner were there, too, and the car was parked in the middle of the next block. There were boxes of Speer Lawman bullets, too, and Felix had a silencer that he'd borrowed from Philip, along with a Leatherman tool he'd taken to carrying on a clip that fit inside his waistband.

"Mostly it's because we haven't found yours. How about a new one?" Felix asked. "We should go down and get one from Franklin's office first thing tomorrow."

"Mine will turn up," Soraya said.

"Let's hope so," Felix said. He looked around the tiny room.

"Have you slept at all?" Soraya asked.

Felix only shook his head. "Not for the last couple of days."

"That's what happens with us when we get into our work," Soraya said.

"Time gets fucked up. We forget to sleep."

"That's right," she said.

"And if I'm not near you . . ." Felix said. He paused. "I don't ever want to be away from you. Never again."

"But . . ." Soraya said.

"Let's not talk about what it means. Not yet. Why don't we listen to some music?"

"All I have here is old Mary J. Blige."

"That's okay," he said. "Let's listen to that."

"I can ask down the hall. There're some white boys from Oklahoma who probably have some Alan Jackson or something. I could get that."

"No," Felix said. "I want to hear what you like."

He stood up and slipped his jacket off and put it on the back of a chair. He reached behind him, checked that the door to the hall was locked. She put on the music, the first MJB album—true old school beats, *What's the 411?*

She gestured at his hat, which he was still wearing. He slipped it off and ran his hand back over his thick greasy hair. She took the hat and put it on her own head.

Felix eased himself down gently on the bed. He slipped behind her and cursed the little mattress and his own big frame.

He said, "We can just take a little rest."

"I think I want you to kiss me."

"I want to," Felix said. "But not now, not yet."

Suddenly she was crying and she folded herself into his lap and seemed unable to stop. He ran his hand through her hair, settled himself against the cinder-block wall. He looked out at the trees and across the street to the windows with their squares of yellow light. There was only the sound of the music playing low and the slow rhythm of her breath as she recovered from her tears.

Franklin sat in his office. It was ten on Friday night. He had Gennardi and Philip watching Simon. Felix was up with Soraya. Jenny was out at a dinner party with her new boss and some people from a magazine called *Radar*. She said she'd call later. So when the phone rang, he figured it was probably Starling, the only other man he knew who was perfectly happy to spend Friday night alone in his office, scheming.

Starling said, "My people on the metro desk tell me that Morris Apple called Lanie Salisbury. He wants to speak to her about his family."

"When's that going down?"

"Tonight at his house. Too bad he said no to a photographer."

"You're really loving your work at the paper these days, aren't you, Starling?"

"Keeps me busy. And if I weren't busy, I guess that would be it for me. I owe you a lot, Franklin."

"Don't think about it," Franklin said.

"I heard from my people that you're happy with a young woman."

Franklin said nothing. He only felt bad for his former father-in-law. He didn't quite know how to explain to him that he wouldn't be remarrying his daughter, which was something that only happened in romance books.

"So if you're happy, I'm happy for you," Starling said.

"And Ellie?" Franklin asked.

"Let's hope she continues to find her own path. I sent her some money. She doesn't want to come back here, so I said that was okay. She'd like to see Felix, though."

"He should visit her. But they talk. She's his mother—what they do is between them."

"True," Starling said. He sounded wistful. "Who did these horrible crimes, anyway?"

"Simon Apple, I'd say. He blames it on his cousin, the whole thing is so traumatic that it forces his father to retire, and then he takes over everything."

"Makes sense. I'll get you an early copy of Lanie's piece."

"Thanks," Franklin said.

"The Apple not falling far from the tree, that's your theory on this? Simon does to his father the same thing his father did to his?"

"I suppose," Franklin said.

"Seems simplistic. But that doesn't make it wrong. I'll be in touch." Starling ended the call.

Franklin leaned back in his desk chair. He pulled out the Magnum. Four and a half pounds. Fifteen inches long. He waved the thing around. The Hogue rubber grip had already begun to mold to his palm. He looked down the length of the barrel. The micrometer click black blade rear sights hadn't been properly adjusted yet, but what difference did it make? It wasn't the sort of gun you'd aim. Just set your feet, hold on tight, and let her roar.

"Bang," he said. "Bang, bang."

But of course there was no one to kill. And with luck, he'd never have to shoot the gun. It was a beautiful thing, though. The satin stainless finish seemed to absorb what little light there was in the room. He found five rounds of Hornady custom ammunition and slipped them in. Now he was equipped to kill the biggest animals North America had to offer. If an insane black bear knocked down his steel front door, he could blow it backward so hard that he'd send it into the dentist's office across the hall. He wished he was stupid enough to take any pleasure in such pointless conjecture. And then his phone rang again, and Franklin set the gun down. He glanced at his caller ID and picked up.

"Eitel Vasquez," he said.

"Angel Pooley stopped talking," Vasquez said. "We hit him, but he's not giving up shit."

"He must've been given an awful lot of money to keep his mouth shut," Franklin said.

"Or they scared him more than I can," Vasquez said.

"Now you're saying 'they.' Why don't you go after this 'they' if you think you know who they are?"

"Orders came down from one of Commissioner Kelly's

lieutenants. We're not watching the Apples. No matter what."

"That's too bad."

"What we need is additional evidence. Substantial evidence. Our guys have a ton of stuff and it points in all different directions. Forensics is a waste of time since we've got a killer arrested. DNA will come through by Tuesday at the latest. But we need a why to drive us through the weekend and we don't have it, and that's pissing me off."

"I'll get you a why," Franklin said.

"If you choose to do that, I'd appreciate it."

"I don't understand."

"There's talk that you're just working for the Apples. Tending to their case. They were using these killings to fight amongst themselves and they're using you to cover them up."

"You believe that?" Franklin asked.

Vasquez was quiet for a moment. Franklin listened for what wasn't there.

"That's why I left the force," Franklin said. "I got tired of detective work being wishful thinking."

"Let me put it another way. Suppose you're not working for the Apples. If you don't clear up your end, you're going to give your Texas husbands an answer that wouldn't give them any more satisfaction than a three-dollar blow job from a crack whore on East Tremont Avenue."

"You ought to know. You going to at least keep this killer at the precinct?"

"Nah. I'm sick of him. We sent him down to the Tombs. He'll go in front of a judge on Sunday morning. But think about this: I hired you to end my grief? You come to me with no motive and a former wash boy called Angel Pooley? I wouldn't pay you a dime."

"You have a funny way of asking for a favor," Franklin said.

"Have a good weekend," Eitel Vasquez said. "Maybe go take your kid for a haircut." And he hung up.

Franklin didn't put the phone down. He dialed Philip and Gennardi and prayed they were in the van and close to Morris's house.

23 Gennardi and Philip were in the middle of an argument when Franklin called. Philip took the call.

Franklin said, "Get over to Morris's house. He's talking to Lanie. If somebody wants to shut that fat boy up, they'll do it now. I'm gonna grab a cab and I'll meet you there."

"Okay," Philip said. He ended the call and told Gennardi where to go.

"The rat gets fat and the house falls apart around him," Gennardi said as he turned right on Madison. "If that story is in every culture, then what makes cultures unique?"

"Manipulation, see? Cooked meat wrapped up in dough is in every culture," Philip said. "But it's a little different everywhere." His voice was creaky from too much arguing. "Parables shift and it's the slight dissension that's interesting. Nobody owns the story of the rat in the house."

Gennardi rolled down the window and spat into the street. He said, "I'm not saying they do, see? I'm saying that we're all the same. Because we're all existing within one big culture, there's no difference between us."

"No way. We're completely different. Go see your wife. Ask her if ravioli and fried pork dumplings taste the same."

"Ah, shit, Philip. Go back to your own country."

"Come with me and I'll sell you to the starving white farmers. Smart guy like you could work the fields in place of an ox."

"At least when I come to the end of a row of cabbages, I know when to turn around."

Philip laughed. "That's about all you're good for."

Gennardi dropped his speed down to nothing. A black BMW shot around them and stopped short in front of Morris's door.

"Huh," Gennardi said. He drifted forward. A man in a suit jumped out of the back of the BMW.

"Simon," Philip said. "I wonder what's the matter."

Gennardi's phone rang. It was Felix. He said, "Lanie just called me from the bathroom at Morris Apple's house. She says Morris is freaking out and she's scared. You guys are near there?"

"We're on it," Gennardi said as he double-parked behind Simon's BMW. "Did she say why he was freaking out?"

"Apparently Morris thinks Simon is coming over there to kill him."

Gennardi threw the phone in the van and checked the rounds in his Glock 9. Philip came around from the other side, his Desert Eagle held loosely in his right hand.

From the other end of the block Gennardi and Philip could see Franklin running toward them from Madison, his bald white head bobbing up and down like a buoy in a dark sea.

Gennardi turned to the front door, which was being closed by Morris's employee. Gennardi waved the gun at him. Leave it open. Franklin reached them.

"Apparently Lanie's got a story she can't handle."

The three men went through the front door. They followed the screaming. In the overwrought front living room, where every surface had an art book or a piece of cut glass on it, Morris Apple was carefully pulling himself out of the fireplace. His back was smoldering. He'd managed to grab an andiron by its coolest point and he waved it around. It looked like Simon had come in and thrown his cousin into the fireplace, where a log had been burning brightly. Unfortunately, Morris had put out the fire and come out with a weapon.

"You don't have a story to tell," Simon Apple yelled. "Nobody is trying to kill you."

"Looks like you just took a shot," Franklin said. Simon turned around. He didn't seem to see Gennardi or Philip. Only Franklin. Simon brandished a little gun, a Sig Sauer P232, and pointed it at Franklin. He shot as Franklin slipped out the Magnum. But the shot was high and did little but blow a hole in the plaster between two paintings. As Simon tried to gain his balance and take another shot, Franklin aimed. He released the Magnum too fast and the shot was low. It blew a hole the size of a melon in the floor at Simon's feet. Simon dropped his little gun.

"I wasn't aiming at you," Simon said.

"Okay," Franklin said. He was hefting the Magnum. "Trigger's a little hairy," he said, half to himself.

"A little?" Philip asked.

Simon said, "We told you he arranged for those killings. He's trying to destroy this family. Why didn't you arrest him?"

"I'm a detective," Franklin said, "not a beat cop. Morris, why don't you put that thing down? There's a lot of art in this room. You don't want to trash any of your nice pictures."

"Who are you?" Morris asked.

"I think I just said who I am," Franklin said. "Now, you've just been attacked, haven't you?"

Morris nodded. He turned and bent down and carefully placed the andiron back in the fireplace. Then he took several steps away from his cousin.

"He wants to kill me," Morris said.

"Oh, for goodness sake, you're such an actor, Morris," Simon said.

"Do you want him arrested for assault?" Franklin asked. He nodded. Say yes.

"Yes," Morris said.

"Great, I'll call some cops. But you've got to say you invited us in. This gunplay, it's not part of your story."

"Sure, I'll say whatever you want. Just get him the hell away from me," Morris said. And then he started to cry. There was the faint sound of a door unlocking and Lanie walked into the room. Her smile belonged on a Wheaties box.

"Well, well, well," she said.

"It's not your story yet," Franklin said.

"Who says?" she asked.

"Starling owns your paper. Last time I checked, he won't print a story till it's true."

"Fuck," Lanie said. "Hanging out with you Novaks is constantly disappointing."

Franklin took a seat on the couch in front of the fireplace. The room was warm and there was a bottle of wine. He lay back on the cushions and stretched out, put his feet up on a marble side table.

"Assault?" Simon said. "That's all you'll get. And he'll drop the charges. You're really making a mess of your assignment."

"Maybe I am," Franklin said. "But like I've been trying to tell you, you're not my client."

"I can't use any of this?" Lanie asked.

"You can put it in your diary," Franklin said. "But I'll make sure Starling won't let it in his newspaper."

Then there was nothing to do but wait. Felix called Franklin and they talked for a moment. They agreed to meet the following afternoon.

Philip walked around the room, admiring the art. He stood in front of a small, dark painting of a man in a pointed hat who held a knife to his chest.

"Christ, that's a Delacroix," he said.

"What's it worth?" Gennardi asked.

"Gennardi, you are absolutely the worst sort of philistine," Philip said. "I—"

"Enough," Franklin said. "You two go home. You did good work here, now leave each other alone."

"Mind if I take the van?" Gennardi said to Philip. "I haven't seen my kid in a while."

"Are you kidding?" Philip said, and laughed. "Tell your wife I remain in awe of her formidable strength of character."

But Gennardi had already gone out the door.

"Still no confession from Simon?" Soraya asked. They'd eaten some pizza they'd gotten at Why Not Call It Ray's on Broadway, and now they were back in her dorm room. Soraya sat on the bed and Felix had the desk chair.

"No. Probably not tonight. Maybe tomorrow," Felix said. He looked around the little room. His back hurt from how he was trying to hold Soraya without falling off the bed. There was no way he could sleep there. And he wasn't even sure she'd let him.

"Did we ever check out of the Sutherland?" Felix asked.

"No."

"I can't imagine a safer place in the world than there tonight. Would you stay there with me?"

Soraya didn't answer. Someone went down the hallway on what sounded like a skateboard. They slapped doors as they went by and when they slapped Soraya's, she cried out. She put one hand on Felix's arm and grabbed his gun with the other. But it slipped out of her hand and fell on her Freitag book bag.

"Yeah, okay," she said. "I'll go with you."

They took a cab across town and in only a few minutes they were back in the presidential suite. They looked out at Central Park. Felix held Soraya's hand.

"I'm sure Morris is in his bed right now, shivering under the covers even though Simon and Angel Pooley are in jail," Felix said.

"His nightmares aren't ever going to go away."

"We know too much about that."

Soraya shrugged. "I guess so. Felix, it meant a lot to me when you took me to my father's grave."

She turned to him and she had an expression he hadn't seen on her face before. She was biting her lips. She looked tentative.

He said, "I can't sleep unless you're near me. I can't even lie still. I may have changed, but . . . I never knew I could need someone so badly."

She said, "I wasn't ready before. But now I'm ready. Let's go in the other room."

They opened the massive French doors and went into the bedroom. They sat on the edge of the bed. Felix kissed Soraya, slowly at first. They fell back on the bed. Their coats were still on.

"Do you want anything?" he asked. "Water or less light?"

"Just don't stop," she said. "Take off your boots. I want to do the rest."

She stood up. She took off her coat and dropped it on the floor. She unbuttoned the top button of her jeans. The dim red light from the living room cast her in silhouette. Felix was propped up on the bed, watching her.

"I feel like I've been thinking about you for the longest time," Felix said. "But I didn't know I'd never be happy till I was with you. Let me see you."

"I want you to see everything," she said. "But I need us to go incredibly slow."

24 Tom Stowe and Ed Wallingford stood at the bar at PJ Clarke's at twelve-thirty on Saturday afternoon. Franklin came in, bristling from the cold wind that had followed him down Third Avenue from his apartment.

"Hello, Ed, Tom," Franklin said. They were near the front entrance. Both men had steaming cups of coffee in front of them and cheeseburgers on white plates. Their food was untouched, though. A bartender stood a few feet from them. He was reading the *Spectator.*

"Piece on the Apple boys in there," Franklin said. "The accusations are flying, but nobody knows how it'll pan out."

"The wicked are only separated after death," Ed Wallingford said. Then, before any more words were exchanged, Ed produced a check and handed it across to Franklin. He said, "That's a cashier's check made out by Bank of New York. We're grateful to you. The case ended when a confessed murderer spent his last night in a cell."

Franklin didn't glance at the check. He laid it on the bar. The bartender came up and he ordered hot tea with plenty of lemon.

Franklin said, "His last night?"

"Angel Pooley died in the Tombs sometime after midnight. He asphyxiated himself. Shoved a T-shirt down his throat and stopped breathing."

"Where'd you hear this?"

"Our friends in the department. But you helped put him there. We know there'll be ongoing trouble with the Apple family. But we're tired. We don't want any part of those people. We want to go home and bury our wives."

The bartender set down Franklin's tea. Franklin put his

hand over the hot water and felt the steam. The cashier's check remained between them.

Franklin said, "I don't feel like I've done what you asked me to do."

"You have, and then some," Ed Wallingford said. "This killing had nothing to do with our wives or our business in Texas. It was happenstance. Pure tragedy. We're not looking forward to living with that, but our wives' deaths are not a result of what we've done in our own lives, and that was what we had to know." Ed Wallingford reached over and took a bite out of his cheeseburger.

"You get a lot of ducks up there at Dykeman's Cross?" Franklin asked.

"Quite a few. That place is deluxe. What you can't eat, they pack up in dry ice and send to your home. It's real nice. Doesn't help much with the grieving, though," Ed said. Franklin watched him glance at Tom. Tom's face was red from windburn, and he seemed determined to speak even less than usual. He clasped his large hands around his coffee cup and looked across the bar at his reflection in the mirror there. But he showed no sign of pleasure or recognition.

"I'm sorry for that," Franklin said. "There's no easy time coming for a long while after someone you love dies."

"No," Ed said. "We know that. But we're grateful to you. We know you'll see this through to its end. Drop us a line, won't you, and tell us how it all worked out?"

"I sure will," Franklin said. "I guess I'd be insulting you if I said I wouldn't like to take this check till then."

"That's so," Ed said.

"All right," Franklin said. He took a sip of the tea. "I'll be going."

Tom Stowe took a step away from the bar. He reached out and shook Franklin's hand. He said, "Thank you. You take care of your people."

"I will," Franklin said. He turned and went back out to the windy, quiet avenue.

Franklin found Felix in the White Fox Lounge on East Ninety-ninth Street. Felix was at the bar, where he was drinking a Coke and watching *SportsCenter.* The place was quiet, but it wasn't empty.

Felix nodded at his father.

Franklin said, "I need to pay you."

"Not yet."

"Lesson number two, after patience. Don't make it about the money."

"I'm with that," Felix said. "I just don't have a bank account yet."

"You're too quick. I need to think of a lesson three."

"How about, It ain't over till it's over?"

"No, I'll do better than that. Vasquez is going to bring us in to see Simon. It's his way of saying thanks."

They walked the long blocks down to the Nineteenth Street Precinct.

"Soraya's okay?" Franklin asked.

"If she's not with me, she's with Edwige. She's okay."

"What's happening between the two of you?"

"I'm not ready to talk about it," Felix said. And Franklin smiled.

Eitel Vasquez met them in the hall in front of the interrogation room. Because it was Saturday he was in weekend clothes, which were Reeboks, baggy black sweatpants, and a green Jets sweatshirt.

"Hey, look," Franklin said, "it's kindergarten cop."

Vasquez didn't seem to hear. He was thumbing through a binder filled with incident reports.

"By the way," Vasquez said. "They ran ballistics on the bullet that took out Gus Moravia. It came out of a Glock 33. That's just a little girl gun. You know anyone who would have a gun like that?"

"No," Franklin said. "I don't."

But Franklin and Felix exchanged a glance.

They went into the interrogation room. This time, in addition to Simon Apple, the four chairs, and a table, there was a steel cart with bagels and fish, hot coffee, and an assortment of soft drinks. There was even a platter with cookies and thick slices of cheesecake. Franklin glanced at Vasquez, raised an eyebrow.

"Compliments of his lawyers," Vasquez said.

"You're shitting me?" Franklin asked.

"Nope," Vasquez said. "Simon wants to talk to you alone, which is fine with me. I sit in this room, all I do is stuff my mouth. Try the smoked salmon. Everything's from Eli Zabar's place." Vasquez grabbed a bialy, cream cheese, and a few slices of salmon that were paper thin and ruddy red. Then he walked out.

Simon Apple sat in a chair. His lawyers had brought him fresh clothes, so now he was in Gucci driving shoes, inky black corduroys, and a pink cashmere sweater over a black polo shirt. He appeared to have showered that morning.

"You don't have a lot of time," Simon said.

"How's that?" Franklin asked. Felix went and stood against the window. There was fresh-squeezed orange juice. He poured some into a paper cup.

"I'll be out of here this afternoon. I'm only sticking around on my lawyer's advice, so I look like a victim. Look, let's say *if* I planned something, *if* I were behind some sort of setup, something, say, where I could implicate both my cousin and force my father into retirement, it didn't work. But that's of no consequence. The murderer died last night. We know this."

"So why don't we have much time? Your lawyers put out a spread and leave? What are they, caterers?"

"They'll be here in a few minutes. But nothing I say to you will stand up in court. And there's something that's bothering me," Simon said. Franklin thought he seemed pensive. His voice was far away.

"Three of these killings were—they made sense. One was an accident, pure and simple. Vasquez said they checked and the old lady in the condo had heart failure. Even her family doesn't think she was killed. I was with Gus Moravia the night he was killed. But I didn't kill him. I'd been talking to him, asking him to bring his brand of danger to my hotel bars, and we were negotiating. Maybe I asked him about his drug connections and maybe that troubled him. But I didn't shoot him. I wouldn't know how to do that and I couldn't be bothered."

Franklin and Felix didn't speak. They looked at each other. Felix had one thought—hadn't he been with Soraya for all of that night? He sipped the orange juice and then involuntarily spat it at the wall. No, he hadn't seen her till very late, past 4 A.M. He remembered. She had no alibi. She said someone had taken her gun. But why would that be? Who would know to take it?

"You're right, we don't have much time," Franklin said.

"It was my cousin," Simon said quickly. "Morris thought I had hired Gus to kill him and . . . I'm not saying he was correct. That's irrelevant now. The real killer is dead. But Morris got to him first. Maybe Morris offered him drugs. He certainly has plenty of access to the good stuff. So they met at the Blue Shade and then he took him outside and shot him, you understand that, don't you?"

There was a knock on the door. Then it swung open and two men in tweed jackets and sweaters came in. They carried briefcases and they didn't smile.

One of them said, "Anything that's been said in here has no value. It was coerced and if anything discussed here finds its way into the press or any court papers, our denial will be flat, succinct, and all-encompassing."

"Is there any other way?" Franklin asked. "Come on, Felix."

Felix dropped his paper cup into the trash. He turned to Simon and said, "Thank you." Then he followed his father out the door.

In the hall they walked past Eitel Vasquez, who was talking on a cell phone. He glanced at the Novaks for a second. Then he covered the phone and said, "Hey, waitasecond."

"What's up? We're in a rush," Franklin said.

"You I'm not asking to wait. Felix, I'm on the phone with my daughter here. She says she saw your picture in the paper a while back and she'd like to go out. After all this, I think you're okay. Want her number?"

"Tell her thanks for the compliment, but I got a girl."

"That reporter?" Vasquez asked. "Because with my daughter, you're better off."

"Somebody else," Felix said. "But I tell you what, I'll call you for her information. There's no reason why we can't be friends."

"That's what I like to hear," Vasquez said. "You're accommodating. You'll go far in this city. Not like your old man."

"I'll be in touch," Felix said. And he and his father went out into the street.

"I think Morris used Soraya's gun," Franklin whispered. "Don't you think that?"

"Yes," Felix said. But he looked startled.

Someone called out, "Franklin Novak." The voice was paper thin and creaky, a paper bag blown into an alley. Stuart Apple beckoned to the Novaks from the back of a black Lexus.

"A moment?" Stuart asked.

"I'll wait. I've got to make some calls," Felix said. So Franklin stepped slowly into the car. Stuart scooted over to make room for him. Franklin settled himself and tried to smile at Stuart. Though the day wasn't cold, Stuart wore gloves and a light gray fedora. His black overcoat seemed old, though it showed little sign of wear.

Franklin felt bad for the older man. After all, his son was in jail. Franklin leaned forward. The car smelled of wet wool and steam heat, which reminded Franklin of Stuart's office. He looked at him. He thought, He's owned buildings for so long, he's become one. Instead of a heart he probably has an oil burner, and gas lines for arteries.

"There's a story we have in the real estate game," Stuart said, "where the worst thing you can have is a tenant who thinks he owns the building. He's like the king rat and he thinks everything is his, so what he does is he eats and he eats and pretty soon—"

"The house bursts around him. I've heard it," Franklin said.

"I've failed," Stuart said. "I brought up a king rat. My son thought I murdered my brother. I did not kill him. He killed himself, and we covered it up. Simon's voracious. He's a greedy bastard who tried to capitalize on a group of grisly murders that had nothing to do with my family. He had me believing that my nephew, Morris, committed these horrible crimes. As if that weak-willed boy could scare or hurt anyone besides himself."

"So let him rot in jail," Franklin said.

"He's my son."

"He won't stop until he's declared you incompetent and he has control over everything. That's what this was all about. You know that, don't you?"

"He's my son," Stuart repeated. Franklin nodded. He gently opened the door and put one foot out on the sidewalk.

"I'm sorry for your trouble," Franklin said.

"Money solves so few problems."

"You're wrong there, but when you do get your son back to the office, you might give him a swift smack in the teeth and try to make him do some real work for a living. That'll buy you a few years, maybe."

Stuart angled his head so he could look up at Franklin, who was now standing on the sidewalk. His eyes were terrifically pale.

"I may be calling you," Stuart said, and pulled the door of the car closed.

25

"It'd be better if you were the one to take Morris down," Felix said.

He was on the phone with Soraya. He was in the back of the van with Gennardi next to him. Philip was driving and Franklin sat in the passenger seat. They were idling on Third Avenue and East Seventieth Street, a few blocks below where Soraya was having lunch with Edwige at Swifty's.

"Why?" Soraya asked.

"Because," Felix said. He breathed long. "Because you're the only one he'll let in the house. It won't be coercion. We know he's home. The police have been watching him since his cousin threw him in the fireplace. But they won't do anything."

"All right," Soraya said. "Pick me up in a few minutes. I just want to eat some more of this steak."

"She's at Swifty's," Felix said when he got off the phone. "We bring her over there, she'll take him down."

"So Morris killed Gus," Gennardi said. "But why?"

"We think he did it to pin it on Simon. Because he thought that Simon had asked Gus to kill him. So Morris thought he'd get to him first. He must've figured that everyone would think that Simon killed Gus. Making it happen at an Apple property seemed obvious."

"Why does Soraya need to be involved?"

"I want her to get the confession," Felix said. "Because if she doesn't, we may have a problem. He used Soraya's gun. I think he took it from her. The gun is registered. Come Monday, the cops are going to figure that out."

"Oh, shit," Gennardi said.

"Let that be a lesson to you," Franklin said.

The four men were quiet for a moment. Felix could feel

that they were all thinking the same thing. Morris was Morris. He'd shown nothing but weakness. But where *had* Soraya been the night that Gus Moravia was shot?

"If—," Gennardi said.

"No ifs," Franklin said. "We do this like Felix says."

Felix's phone rang. Soraya.

"I've got a better idea. Pull up to Morris's house in about fifteen minutes. I'm around the corner from there now and I don't need a chauffeur."

"Are you sure you can do this?" Felix asked. "Don't you need a gun?"

There was a pause on the line, a sharp intake of breath.

"No. I can get through this without it."

Because it was Saturday afternoon on Madison Avenue, Soraya found that she had to weave through the rich people as she made her way over to Morris Apple's town house. She'd been out with Edwige and she was dressed up in a short blue skirt, high brown boots, and a long red coat that Edwige had bought her just before lunch. Her black hair was loose and flowing, and more than one man in a Barbour coat and suede penny loafers did a double take as she walked by.

She walked onto East Sixty-third Street and made note of an undercover police car double-parked across from Morris's house. Two officers were talking quietly, their hands in their laps. She couldn't tell if they noticed her. She went up to Morris's door and knocked on it. There was silence. Soon enough, the intercom buzzed. A voice said, "Are you alone?"

"Yes," Soraya said.

The door clicked open. There was no sign of the servant who had greeted her the first time she'd visited. The house was entirely quiet.

"Hello?" Soraya called out. She glanced into the living room, where everything had been put back into place. There was no sound.

"Up here," a voice said through the intercom system.

She went up the stairs and alighted on the second floor, where she hadn't been previously.

"In here," the voice called out. She made her way toward the back of the house. She opened a pair of double doors and stepped into a bedroom that looked like something out of the late nineteenth century. Carpets were strewn about along with tables, daybeds, and a pair of massive wardrobes on either side of the room. In the middle of it all was a gigantic four-poster bed.

Morris was sitting up in a ball in the middle of the bed. He was in a corduroy suit that was a sort of orange-brown and a plain white shirt with a very small collar. He wore his bright red Asics sneakers. He looked up at her.

Soraya's phone rang. Without looking, she took the phone from her left pocket, opened the connection, said, "I'm fine," and ended the call.

"We weren't able to date, were we?" Morris asked.

"I'm afraid not," Soraya said.

"Do you think I did something wrong?"

"Yes. I think you did something wrong. You murdered Gus Moravia. And you used my gun to do it."

"That's not true!" Morris said. He carefully swung his legs around and stood up. "My cousin killed him. That Gus—he refused to kill me, so my cousin killed him. I think I told you that. You don't listen."

"You did it," Soraya said. "You killed him. Felix Novak says he can get a bartender to swear she saw you that night. You killed him. I loved him. And you killed him."

"It isn't so!"

"Give yourself up. There are two policemen across the street and they'll be happy to arrest you."

"I didn't do it."

"Where is my gun?"

"I don't have it," Morris said. "What do you mean, 'Where is my gun'? Oh my Lord, you did it, didn't you? That's what this is about—you're trying to pin it on me." He began to back away from her.

"Morris, everyone knows you can be quite violent. You can admit the crime now, today. And you can go in and have your lawyers deal with the consequences."

"So it's my word against yours."

"Yes," Soraya said. Her voice was entirely cool. She said, "Let's go downstairs now."

And they went down, slowly. Soraya followed Morris, who didn't cry.

"Where is the gun, Morris?" Soraya asked before they opened the front door.

"My left coat pocket," Morris said. "It would've been perfect. I could have pinned that crime on you. But something wouldn't let me."

"It wouldn't have worked is why," Soraya said. She eased her gun out of his pocket. She didn't poke it in his ribs. She opened the front door. "If I were going to kill my boyfriend, I'd have shot him in the heart, not the gut."

26 Later on Saturday evening Franklin was napping when Jenny Hurly used her key to let herself into his apartment. He was on the couch and he righted himself and looked at her. She sat down next to him.

"Good day?"

"Not too bad," Franklin said. He smiled. "We didn't wrap the case up neatly, but it's closed. We tried our best. My people took care of most of the details. What about you?"

"I went shopping. I bought you a new suit. You'll have to go down to Paul Stuart and have it fitted."

"Wow," Franklin said. He walked over to the window.

"Do you want to go out to eat later?"

"Yes," Franklin said. "I got us a table at Elaine's. All of us—Felix, Soraya, Philip, and the Gennardis."

"That sounds nice," Jenny said. But she sounded distracted. She looked around the room.

"There's one other thing," Franklin said.

"What's that?"

"Jenny Hurly, will you marry me?"

Franklin slipped a small blue box out of his pocket. He handed it to Jenny, who opened it. The box contained a diamond engagement ring. She looked down at it.

"Oh, Franklin—yes, yes, I will."

She threw her arms around him and began to cry. They fell down then onto the soft cushions of the couch, and she kissed his bald head and he laughed. Behind them the sun's reflection slowly vanished from the horizon and the lights from the river shimmered in the windows. The barges honked and the traffic rushed along on the East River Drive. Franklin smiled because soon, he'd be married again.

*   *   *

"I wondered," Felix said. "I won't lie to you and say I didn't."

"I know you did. But I didn't kill Gus."

Soraya and Felix were in an Irish bar called Banky's around the corner from Elaine's. They were drinking ice-cold Budweiser and glasses of water. They'd spent the late afternoon in Soraya's dorm room with the lights low, their phones off, and their guns unloaded and field-stripped. They hadn't made love, though. Both had been too shaky, too tense.

Instead they'd talked. Felix admitted that he couldn't even handle the idea of loving her until he'd made peace with his own anger. And they agreed that he'd done that— that he'd made a temporary peace, at least. They talked about loss and about how terribly violent their lives had been and how they'd like to put that behind them. But they didn't speak of the one thing that bothered both of them. Finally, once they'd arrived on the East Side too early and holed up in Banky's, he'd asked her.

He said, "I just had to hear you say it. Morris will probably beat the rap in any case. But the bullet . . ."

"He won't beat it. His servant saw him with my gun."

"Yes, I suppose that's so," Felix said. "We should probably get over to Elaine's. We don't want to keep them waiting. I've got a feeling my father has a big announcement to make."

"You won't believe our good news!" Franklin said.

He gathered Felix and Soraya to him and hugged them. Felix looked beyond his father to Jenny Hurly. She was half standing. Her hair was in ringlets and she seemed slightly formal, in a neat black suit. Behind her Gennardi stood with

Dianne. Lisa was talking with Philip in French, which she was learning in school.

Felix leaned over his father. He said, "You must be Jenny Hurly. I'm happy to finally meet you."

"You too! I guess your father can't keep me a secret any longer," Jenny said. And the announcement was made.

Felix drew Soraya to him while the waiter poured out more wine and gave up trying to get them to order.

Felix whispered, "I love you, Soraya, no matter what."

She kissed him then. No one at the table had seen this, that the city's most beautiful, fated, dangerous pair of young people were actually, really together.

A waiter came and poured champagne. A few regulars arrived at the periphery of the table and pulled up chairs, and they toasted Franklin's engagement. Felix shook hands with everyone before slipping out with Soraya. Behind them the room was washed in storms of laughter and the light reflected in a half dozen champagne glasses held high in the air.

WELCOME TO ALEX MINTER'S
NEW YORK

A perilous playground for the rich, the young and the troubled, and the criminals who prey upon them.

LITTLE SISTER'S LAST DOSE
by Alex Minter

Fueled by black coffee and vengeance, Felix Novak speeds across the country to New York City on a mission to find and kill whoever's responsible for his sister's death. With time against him, Felix must turn to childhood friend Soraya Navarro, and his father, Franklin, a disgraced cop turned P.I.

KILLING COUSINS
by Alex Minter

When the wives of two billionaire Texans are brutally murdered in New York's Sutherland Hotel, Franklin and Felix Novak and Soraya Navarro need to move fast before the killer strikes again. As Franklin's team relentlessly pursues their man, the only things that throw them off track are Felix and Soraya's increasingly complicated relationship and a corpse with a bullet in the belly.

As many as one in three
Americans with HIV...
DO NOT KNOW IT.

More than half of those
who will get HIV this year...
ARE UNDER 25.

HIV is preventable.
You can help fight AIDS.
Get informed. Get the facts.

www.knowhivaids.org
1-866-344-KNOW

Printed in the United States
By Bookmasters